HEARTLESS

HEARTLESS

BY REG IVORY

HEARTLESS

iUniverse books may be ordered through booksellers or by contacting:

iUniverse
1663 Liberty Drive
Bloomington, IN 47403
www.iuniverse.com
1-800-Authors (1-800-288-4677)

ISBN: 978-1-4917-5689-8 (sc)
ISBN: 978-1-4917-5690-4 (hc)
ISBN: 978-1-4917-5688-1 (e)

Library of Congress Control Number: 2014959926

Printed in the United States of America.

iUniverse rev. date: 01/06/2015

For the boy who used to dream and write

T he man carefully reviewed the detailed file at the cheap, cigarette-burned plastic desk in his motel room. Satisfied with the information from his research, he closed the file, snapped open the aluminum briefcase, and removed an expensive-looking black leather wallet. He glanced at the name on the driver's license behind the plastic cover: Thomas Kennedy. It was easy to remember. The address on the license was from Atlanta, Georgia. His photograph was a good likeness. The license had been accepted without question at the car-rental business close by the Clemson airport and at the shabby motel on the outskirts of Pendleton, South Carolina. He had paid in cash, of course.

He looked at the stack of other driver's licenses inside an imitation-leather case. Sorting through them slowly, noting his identical photograph on each one, he reminisced briefly about his other personalities and occupations during his recent visits. After returning the other licenses to the case, he retrieved a long, thin display file of business cards. He turned slowly to the *K* pages and found the "Thomas Kennedy" cards, noting Mr. Kennedy was an attorney from what sounded like a distinguished firm in Atlanta. A prestigious occupation was always helpful. People were impressed with attorneys. They trusted them, despite a multitude of evidence to the contrary. Trust was important in the man's endeavors. He added several Kennedy cards to his wallet.

Finally, he turned to the small mahogany box that held the medals. He opened it carefully and noted the smiling photograph of Henry Clavin inserted prominently in the inside top of the box. The medals had been polished, and they shone brilliantly. He examined each one. He had found them in a dingy pawnshop in Columbia, South Carolina, several months ago—all Vietnam-era campaign medals awarded only to marines or navy personnel. The first was the Combat Action Ribbon. Beside it was the Vietnam Service Medal with three stars, plus a palm tree in the center. He thought the palm tree was a nice touch. And wasn't South Carolina's state tree a palm tree? No, it was a palmetto tree. However, it was close enough to be a good omen. The man believed in omens.

The service medal was the most colorful of the three, and the man knew each star represented a different battle. His research had been detailed. The last medal was the Republic of Vietnam Meritorious Unit Citation for valor. The three medals had one thing in common—the name of the recipient and his hometown had been engraved on the back of each: "Henry Clavin. Pendleton, SC." Most of this information—and a smiling photograph of Clavin—had been supplied by the Department of Defense.

More than three months of research by a private investigator had shown that Mr. Clavin had been an interesting man while he lived. A chronic alcoholic and abuser of both his wife and daughter, Clavin had died in 1978, five years after his return from Vietnam with a less-than-honorable discharge. The man calling himself Thomas Kennedy had hired the private detective to find personal information about Clavin. Apparently, he had seriously abused his wife and daughter, and this fact was well known all over Pendleton. Newspaper stories from that time explained he had hung himself in the bathroom of his home at 57 Somerset Lane. The funeral notice asked that in lieu of flowers, contributions be made to an educational fund for his seven-year-old daughter, Arie. Based on the date of his death, she would be thirty-five now.

Kennedy had also found that after her mother passed away, Arie had lived in the same house with an elderly aunt. When the aunt had died, Arie had remained in the home alone. She had never married. She did not even have a pet. She worked three days a week at a rest home on the outskirts of Pendleton. Tomorrow was not one of her workdays. And she drank a little—a lot, actually.

The man smiled to himself. He was pleased with the research. This would be an easy one. He would catch her early enough in the morning so that the alcohol would not have dulled her mind too much. He needed her clear enough mentally to be able to remember her father—and the things her father had done to her. And if her memories were not as sharp as he needed them to be, he would remind her. His investigation had been detailed and accurate. His own depraved parents had taught him a great deal about personal abuse. He wondered if they would approve of the way he was using their substantial wealth. It would not be hard to manipulate someone with Arie's background into hysteria. He had practiced this art to perfection many times before.

He returned the medals to their box and to the aluminum case. Snapping it closed, he decided to turn in early and get a good night's sleep. He always did better when he slept well. In the morning, he would check out and have a big breakfast at the restaurant down the street. Then, at about ten o'clock, he would drive over to 57 Somerset Lane to see how much little Arie could remember about her father.

He shivered in anticipation and then walked slowly over to the bed. His first act after checking in had been to strip the bed and then carefully remake it with his own personal silk sheets. They were dark red, almost purple. He switched on the bed lamp, lay down on his back, smiling, and reached over to turn on the tape recorder beside him. He would listen again to his visit with Gladys Hardin from a month or so ago. Gladys had not noticed that the glass she filled with milk for her grandson contained a dozen sharply pointed thumbtacks. The boy had gulped the milk down and then begun to choke and strangle, blood pouring from his mouth. Gladys described things vividly. She was extremely distraught, and the newspaper story of her loss of control at the funeral was what had attracted Kennedy to her. Their time together had not gone well at first but had become extremely rewarding toward the end. He reminded himself to turn down the sound just before Gladys started screaming. Then he turned out the light and began to touch himself—slowly at first and then more rhythmically, rapidly.

He slept well.

2.

"-**H**omes, where's the toilet paper?" Jack Novak hit his head on the bathroom cabinet and swore.

"Whaddaya need that for, Jackie?" Homes laughed. "Use that old *Playboy*."

"Put it on the list." Jack looked at himself in the mirror. His midforties were beginning to show. The drinking hadn't helped. The brown hair was thinning a little. His teeth looked okay, maybe a little yellow. Was he putting on some weight?

"What list?" Homes yelled from the living room.

"The grocery list, you nitwit." Jack couldn't help but smile at his best friend's indifference to mundane housekeeping chores. They had decided to move in together after working a strange murder case about a year ago. Sergeant Homes Kenney still had a few years to go before retirement from the Roswell, Georgia, police department. Then he would join Jack at his private-investigation firm. They were former partners on the force, and their friendship had spanned more than ten years now. Each one had bailed the other out of numerous bad situations. Their back-and-forth exchange of feigned insults and well-intentioned humor was a permanent part of a longtime close relationship.

"That's the beer list, Jack, my man," Homes answered, "not that you're interested."

Jack was a recovering alcoholic who was approaching a year of sobriety. Homes had helped him through some tough times, and humor was his way of gauging Jack's mood. Jack walked into the living room with a can of Tab.

"How can you drink that shit, Jack? I thought they stopped making Tab."

"I find it every couple of months. It tastes different."

"Yeah, it's different because of all the chemicals that're screwing up your system."

"My system is fine. You're the one that's screwed up."

"Oh yeah? I guess you didn't know you're rooming with a computer genius."

Jack laughed. "Who? You? Those computer searches you do for the world's best beer and the Russian bride website don't count, you know."

"Hey, I'm glad you reminded me. You know Bob Stacy down at the station?"

"Sure, I know Bob."

"Well, he hooked up with some Russian broad on that bride website, and she arrived about four weeks ago."

"You're shittin' me."

"No, seriously. He brought her by the station last week, and she's a real honey. Got those big Russian boobs, big smile, big ass."

Jack laughed again. "So she's perfect, huh?"

"Well, not exactly. Stacy says their biggest problem is communication."

"What does he mean?"

"See, she only knows two English sentences. One of 'em is 'I hungry.' The other one is 'I want to fuck.'"

"Don't tell me Stacy is complaining about that."

"Oh no. The problem was the way she pronounced it. She said, 'I want to *fook*.'"

"Fook?"

"Yeah. At first, Stacy had no idea what she meant. He met her at the airport, picked up her bag, and the first thing she says is 'I want to fook.' They get back to his place, and she tells him again, 'I want to fook.' Stacy is scratching his head and trying to show her he doesn't know what she means. He shows her the bathroom, and she shakes her head. He takes her to the kitchen, and that ain't it either. The broad is getting madder and madder."

"You're making this up."

"I am not. So finally, she goes into the bedroom, takes off all her clothes, lies down, and points to her snatch—which Stacy says is bright red, by the way—and she says again, 'I want to fook.'"

"And does Stacy get it this time?"

"Oh yeah, he gets it *big*-time! They've been fooking ever since."

"Homes, I think you're full of shit."

"I'm giving it to you straight, buddy. You can ask Stacy."

"So this is a match made in heaven."

"Again, not exactly. Every day, when Stacy gets home from work, he opens the door, and she's standing there saying, 'I want to fook.' Ordinarily, Stacy would be glad to hear this. But he's starting to work longer hours just so he doesn't have to listen to her. Another thing—she likes to watch television, but if the show bores her, she says either 'I hungry' or 'I want to fook.' Stacy says sometimes he'd just like to have a regular conversation—not that he's complaining, mind you."

Jack shook his head. "So is he going to keep her or send her back to Russia? How does this shit work?"

"I think she's got ninety days or something like that. Oh, she's got one other problem."

"Here it comes; I knew there had to be something else. What is it?"

"Well, she drinks a little."

"How much is a little?"

"She kills a bottle of vodka every two days or so. Depends on how much time they spend fooking."

"Now, you're making up that last part."

"Not the drinking," Homes said, laughing. "She won't drink any of that cheap vodka that you used to drink either. She wants some of that fancy Russian shit. Stacy says it's way too expensive."

"So he's weighing the cost of vodka against all that fooking."

"That's about right." Homes took a good look at his friend and liked what he saw. Jack had been dry and on the wagon for some time now, and they talked about it openly.

"Hey, you still seeing that psychiatrist?" Homes knew that Jack had begun attending AA meetings again. But the psychiatrist visits were new for Jack, and Homes felt they were a sign that Jack was serious this time about staying sober.

"Yep. See her this afternoon, as a matter of fact."

"So it's a *her*, is it? And does this serious medical procedure take place on a couch?"

A pillow missed Homes by a foot.

"As a matter of fact, we both sit in chairs—separate chairs, you moron."

"Like Tony Soprano used to do, huh?"

"Yeah, only our conversations aren't so nasty."

"So what have you found out about yourself so far, Jack, my boy?"

"Laura—that's Dr. Benjamin—says that I didn't hate my mother or father and that I wasn't pissed off because I was an only child. Oh, and I was never groped by a priest when I was an altar boy."

"And this is costing you how much—one hundred eighty dollars an hour?"

"One hundred eighty-five."

"But didn't you know all that shit about yourself before?"

"Yes, but it's opening doors to my psyche."

"Your what?"

"My psyche, you dumb cop. By clearing up these details from my past, we can dig deeper into all my other shit."

Homes shook his head and decided to antagonize Jack a bit more. "Now, Jackie, you wouldn't be considering, uh, digging deeper into Laura the psychiatrist, would you, buddy?"

They both laughed, and Jack readied another pillow.

"Describe this Laura to me, Jack." Homes had a know-it-all smirk on his face.

"She's very intellectual."

"Don't give me that shit. What does she look like? I want to hear about legs and ass and boobs."

"She has them all, Detective Kinney. Some in abundance."

"Now, that's what I want to hear. Tell me about the abundance."

"Well"—Jack seemed deeply buried in thought—"she has a lot of hair."

This time, three pillows sailed through the air at Jack.

3.

L aura Benjamin glanced at her notes and then at her patient, Jack Novak.

"So what have we learned about ourselves today, Jack?"

Jack smiled at his psychiatrist. "Isn't the question really what have *you* learned about *me*?"

"These sessions are supposed to be about personal insight, Jack," she said. "I'm more interested in what you think."

Jack considered this for a moment as he looked at his doctor. He liked her well-groomed appearance. She never had a brunette hair out of place. She went easy on the makeup. She was professionally but attractively dressed. She had nice legs, a great shape, and no obvious bad habits. Over almost four months, he had grown to trust Laura's guidance and patience as he'd tried to make some sense of his behavior, primarily his drinking as well as his being drawn to troubled women. That certainly wasn't the case with Laura. Other than an aversion to using the Internet only for e-mail, she didn't seem to be bothered about anything.

"Doc, can I ask you a personal question?"

"Of course."

"Is it true that your, ah, ethical code, or whatever you psychiatrists call it, prevents you from having personal relationships with your patients?"

It was Laura's turn to smile. "Yes, it does. And what's this all about?"

"Just what it sounds like. I'd like to be able to see you outside this office. I think they call it dating. But it's been so long I may have forgotten."

Laura turned serious. "Jack, I don't think that's a good idea—for a couple of reasons. First of all, I don't feel you've thoroughly explored the reasons for your attraction to certain types of women who may not be, well, right for you. And beginning a relationship outside our sessions would mean you'd have to see a different psychiatrist, and that could be an unwise thing at this point."

"Tell me the truth, Doc," Jack said, smiling. "You know about my Bobby Darin fetish, and you think I'm weird." Jack's fondness for old Darin recordings was well known to his friends and something he had mentioned to his doctor in passing.

Laura laughed this time. "The Darin thing is suspicious, but that's not the problem. The problem is what would be best for you."

"Hey, I look on the bright side, Doc. Haven't you been telling me to bring more positive things into my life?"

"So I have. So I have. Jack, to be serious for a moment, what do you think is the most positive thing about your life right now? What is it that keeps you focused and engaged?"

"That's easy," Jack said. "It's my work. Working on a tough case. Being able to solve puzzles, to deal with someone else's problems."

"I agree. So what are you working on right now?"

Jack took a deep breath. "Nothing much right now. A couple of divorce cases that will have a good monetary payout. But nothing heavy, nothing that's forcing me to dig deep and get involved."

Laura nodded. "And haven't we found out that when you reach these periods—let's call them humdrum periods for the moment—when you find yourself not being challenged, isn't this when your personal problems begin?"

"I think we both know that's true," Jack agreed.

"Then perhaps what you need is a tough case to take on and engage yourself in before you take on a new girlfriend."

They stared at each other for a moment. "Does that mean you're not completely against the girlfriend thing?"

They both laughed, and the doctor shook her head. "Have you got any new cases that you feel may put that inquisitive mind of yours to work?"

"Not really. But I can dig up some old files. And maybe Homes can find something interesting."

Laura glanced at her watch and stood up. "Why don't we do this? See what you can find in terms of a new case. I'll think about the, ah, girlfriend thing and talk to some of my friends in the profession. There are some outstanding psychiatrists in the Atlanta area. Actually, I want to think this whole thing through very carefully. So should you."

"What's there to think about, Doc? All you've got to do is develop a love for Bobby Darin, and we're a perfect match!"

4.

The man who called himself Thomas Kennedy glanced at the house at 57 Somerset Lane. It had seen better days. But so had everything else in Pendleton, South Carolina. When they'd closed the army base in 1980, everything about the town had seemed to slowly disintegrate. As he drove past to make certain there was no one out on the street, Kennedy noted that the turn-of-the-century brownstone had not been cared for—another good indication about the state of mind of the owner. The grass on the lawn had long ago turned brown and weedy. The porch, painted gray at one time, was cracked and peeling. One shutter of indeterminate color hung loosely from an old hinge. The others needed work too. Kennedy trusted that the house was a reflection of the battered, hopefully even tortured, soul of Arie Clavin.

He parked two doors down from 57 in his plain black rental sedan and then checked his file and box of medals in the aluminum briefcase. He carefully switched on the tiny voice-activated tape recorder he had loaded with fresh batteries and tested that morning. Finally, he put on a pair of thin leather gloves, took a deep breath, and got out of the car.

He walked slowly down to 57, preparing his best self-assured smile. People were more apt to trust and confide in others who smiled. Mr. Kennedy did not often smile, but he had practiced before a mirror until he felt he projected just the right image of trustworthiness. Putting troubled people quickly at ease had been the secret to his past successes. Climbing up the seven shabby stairs to the porch, Mr. Kennedy could hear a television inside the house. He would ask Arie to turn it off before he began. Interruptions were not good. He needed her full attention.

He knocked at a moderate level and waited patiently. Listening to the movement inside, he flushed slightly with anticipation.

The door stuck stubbornly and would not open easily. When it did, Mr. Kennedy was pleased with what he saw. Arie Clavin looked much older than her midthirties. She appeared to be at least fifty. She wore a stained housecoat and no makeup. There was a small, angry-looking red scab on her left cheek. Her hair might have been an attractive shade of auburn at one time, but that had been long ago. She was short and overweight, and she smoked. The yellow cigarette stains on her fingers told Mr. Kennedy that she did quite a bit of smoking. And he could smell alcohol. He would have to work more quickly than he had planned.

"Pardon me," he began. "Are you *Mrs.* Arie Clavin?" he asked, making the purposeful error.

"It's *Miss* Clavin. Whatever it is you're selling, I don't want any." Arie took a deep drag on her cigarette and started to close the door.

"Oh, excuse me, Miss Clavin," Kennedy said, reaching for his wallet. "I'm not a salesman. I'm an attorney. I'm here to speak to you about a matter than concerns your father, Henry Clavin, now deceased, I believe." He handed her his card and practiced his sincere smile again.

"You're goddamn right he's deceased." She reached up to rub the scab. "Damn near thirty years now—may his soul rot in hell. Good and dead." Arie looked briefly at the card. "I don't want any part of that old bastard." She started to close the door again.

"Oh, Miss Clavin, I apologize. I should have explained. I have something from your father's estate—some personal items that, may I say, will be of significant interest to you." Kennedy nodded at his briefcase.

"Estate? What the hell? That scumbag didn't have no estate. Besides, he died thirty years ago." She paused and looked up at the slender, well-dressed, smiling man before her. "Is it money?" Her eyes took on a different hue as she licked her lips.

Kennedy smiled at her and to himself. He had her!

"These items are of real value, Miss Clavin—I can promise you that. As to their potential monetary worth, that would have to be determined. Would it be possible for me to come inside? This really isn't a matter I should discuss publicly out here."

Arie looked the man over one more time, took another pull on her cigarette, and widened the doorway for him. Kennedy entered the house and waited for Arie to lead him into the living room. An unpleasant odor prevailed—a mixture of decay, alcohol, and nicotine. Every piece of furniture in the living room was covered crookedly with a soiled sheet. There were solid oak rafters across the ceiling. He would need those rafters later. Kennedy stood patiently, waiting for her invitation to sit down.

"What did you say your name was?" Arie asked, walking into a large, dimly lit room. She lit another cigarette from the stub in her hand and then reached for the tall glass on a well-ringed table as she balanced herself on the arm of the sofa.

"Kennedy. Thomas Kennedy. From the firm of Olden, Stormwell, and Kennedy in Atlanta. Perhaps you've heard of us?" He smiled a perfect smile at her.

"I don't know a damn thing about lawyers. Why don't you sit over there?" She motioned toward another of the sofas as she placed his business card on the table. Her voice was beginning to sound thick and slurred. He would have to hurry.

"Thank you, Miss Clavin. You have a lovely home."

"Not what it used to be. Only me now. Don't have time to ... Say, would you like a drink?" She walked unsteadily into the adjacent kitchen.

"How kind of you. Thank you, but not right now. May I turn off the television while we talk?" He pushed the power button. Mr. Kennedy had purposely never tasted alcohol, but he had studied all about it as well as many other drugs, and he was an expert on their adverse effects on human beings.

From the kitchen, Arie yelled back at him. "Yeah. Sure. Hey, if you need to use the bathroom, you'll have to go out here in the back. I don't use the, uh, bathroom off the living room there. It's ... it's out of order. Hey," she said, beginning again, "what's all this shit about my father's estate? You have a check?"

"No, it's not a check, Miss Clavin," Kennedy replied. "It's something much more personal—something that will bring back many memories of your father, I'm sure." He opened the briefcase beside him and made certain the recorder was operating as she walked back into the room.

"I don't need any more goddamn memories of that bastard," she said, seating herself across from him and scratching the scab on her cheek. It began to bleed. She had brought a bottle of gin back with her from the kitchen, and she placed it on the table. "It's hard enough to forget as it is. You don't have no idea." She paused to take a long drink and waved her arm. "That man. He was a devil."

"A devil?" Kennedy asked, warming to his task. "That's a strange way to speak about your father. Perhaps you would be good enough to tell me a little more about him—for our files. After all, I am an attorney. Everything is confidential." Kennedy paused to smile again at the drunken woman. "Now, what could your father have done that was so bad?" He bent forward toward her.

"True. All true. You don't know. Nobody knows since she died. Dead. My mother. Wasn't much better. She let him. She—" Arie stopped and took another drag.

"Your mother," Kennedy said softly. "Tell me more about your mother."

"No one knows. No real mother to me. She—she let him do it. She let him." Arie took another long drink and stared at the floor.

"Do it? Do what, Miss Clavin?" Kennedy shivered slightly at what he knew was coming. "You can tell me."

"Goddamn bastard." Her fingers moved to the scab again. "Would come in my room at night. Anytime he wanted. Could smell him. She never said a goddamn word. I would call her. 'Momma? Momma?' Never answered. Never. Even when I screamed." Arie began to sob as she took another drink.

"When did he start, Arie? You can tell me. Take your time."

"Start? When he … I was a kid. Small. A goddamn kid. What did I know? I … He said he was my father and I had to let him." Arie wiped her face on the sleeve of her housecoat, smearing the blood on her cheek.

"You were quite young?" Kennedy filled her glass.

"Young? I was—yeah, I was young." Arie's voice became strident. "Goddamn right I was young. Maybe four or five. Before he left."

"Left? Your father left? But where did he go?" Kennedy knew what she was going to say.

"He left for the goddamn war. Vietnam. The war." Arie started to laugh hysterically. "Everyone hated that war. Not me. Not li'l ole Arie. The war saved Arie. Yes, it did. Saved by a war." Her choked laughter slowly ended, and she took another drink.

"And then he came back, didn't he, Arie?" Kennedy slowly withdrew the box of medals from the briefcase.

"Back, yeah. Over. The goddamn war was over." The scab on her face bled freely now as she continued to scrape it with her nails. "They all—everyone was happy. Not ole Arie. And not Arie's momma. No, sir. We weren't happy at all." She pronounced the last two words emphatically again. "*At all*."

"Your mother?" Kennedy prompted her as he opened the box in his lap.

"Mother, my ass. Not much a one. Not much of my mother. She would let him. Let him do it. Told me later it was so he would leave her alone." Arie took another long sip. "He came to me instead of to her. Never even said she was sorry."

Kennedy licked his lips. Small beads of sweat appeared on his forehead. "Did she ever tell you what he did to her, Arie?"

Arie sobbed and wiped her face again. "What he did ... What he did—he did the same things. Those same things. With his hands. Only now, it was worse. His hands were—they went all over li'l Arie. Seven. I was only five or seven, goddamn it. Didn't know. Only knew it hurt. Hurt so bad. So bad." Arie broke down entirely now. "God, it hurt. How could—how could he hurt his li'l girl so bad?"

It was time. Kennedy put the open medal box on the table and turned it toward the miserable woman. The photo of Henry Clavin inside the top of the box smiled up at Arie. What had she called him? A devil? Yes. The devil and the daughter—reunited.

"Look, Arie. Look at what he wanted you to have. Look at your father."

The drunken woman strangled a sob and looked up, seeing the box on the table before her.

"What's ... What? That box?"

Kennedy knew his voice sounded tender and sympathetic. "It's your father, Arie. Your father. Look at how he's smiling at you. At you, Arie. At his baby daughter."

Arie reached out tentatively to the box and then pulled her hand back as if she had almost touched a snake. "It's him. He's—it's him." She stared in disbelief at the box.

"Yes, Arie. It is him. He's back, Arie."

"Back? What? Back? Dead. He's dead. Gone. Dead." She reached up to the scab and rubbed again, smearing bloody streaks on her cheek.

"Not in spirit, Arie," Kennedy said soothingly, almost hypnotically. "In spirit, he's back with you. Can't you feel his presence? He's here again, Arie."

"Feel? Can't feel. No. Don't want. No." The woman struggled for reality, sobbing, choking, as she stared at her father's smiling picture in the box.

Kennedy sensed this was the moment. "Can you feel his hands, Arie? Can you smell his breath? He's drunk again, isn't he?"

"Always. Always drunk. Pushing me. Slapping. Pull me over. Laughing. His hands." Arie's voice rose steadily until she spoke almost in falsetto. "Those hands. Touch me. Don't touch me no more."

"Yes, Arie. His hands are touching you. Everywhere." Kennedy's voice was hoarse as he whispered. His eyes gleamed as he looked at the pathetic woman.

"No. Noooo."

Kennedy sensed he could push her a little further. "Yes. Yes, Arie. He's here. He's back. Daddy's back with you."

The woman struggled to her feet, swaying. Her housecoat was wide open, revealing her grotesque body. Kennedy shuddered at the sight. She knocked her glass from the table, and it shattered on the floor. "Momma!" she shouted. "Momma, he's back. He's come back, Momma." She stumbled across the shabby living room to the old bathroom door, its chipped white paint yellowed with age.

Kennedy followed her every move with his eyes, licking his lips with anticipation.

His hands dropped to his lap and moved up and down across his thighs.

"Momma!" she cried, opening the door to the bathroom. "Momma, please help me this time. Please. Don't let him. Don't." The door slammed behind her. She began to scream.

Slowly, Kennedy stood, picked up the tape recorder, increased the recording volume, and set it on the floor outside the bathroom door. In a singsong voice, he began to call out to her softly. "Arie. Little Arie. It's Daddy, Arie. Daddy's home to play."

The woman's sobs and screams increased. "No. Noooo!"

Kennedy moved his hands across the bathroom door, the thin leather gloves still allowing him to scratch loudly. "Arie, it's Daddy's hands. Hear them? Feel them? Let Daddy in, Arie. Daddy needs you."

The woman behind the door was uncontrollably hysterical. She gagged and choked in between screams and sobs. Animal noises came from her mouth. Then she became sick to her stomach.

As he listened to the frenzied woman, Kennedy glanced at his watch. He had spent too much time already, and that was always dangerous. He would have to finish quickly.

"Arie." He began to whisper again. "Arie, it's Daddy." He scratched again on the bathroom door. "I'm not going away, Arie. Daddy will always be here for you. I have a present for you, Arie. A present from Daddy." He moved his hands around the door again, listening to another burst from the terror-filled woman. Satisfied, he walked over to his briefcase and withdrew a ten-foot length of thick, strong red nylon rope. He had formed one end into a noose. Kennedy preferred to think of it as a halo—a halo over Daddy's little angel, over little Arie's head.

He picked up the half-empty bottle of gin, walked back to the door, scratched it again, and heard a muffled cry. "Arie, let Daddy in now so I can give you your present. You're going to like it, Arie. It's your favorite color—red." The sobbing continued behind the door.

"It's time to play, Arie. Play with your new present. Open the door, Arie, or I'll be very mad. And you know how I get when I'm mad, Arie."

The sobs increased as he heard movement behind the door and the click of the lock. He opened the door and found Arie sitting on the floor, barely conscious.

"Thank you, Arie. Now you and Daddy can play." He handed her the gin bottle and glanced up at the rafters running across the bathroom ceiling. From the newspaper stories he had read of Henry Clavin's death, Kennedy knew this was where the man had committed suicide. How fitting—and ironic—that Clavin and his daughter would be reunited this way.

Quickly, he tossed an end of the red rope over one of the rafters and pulled it so that the noose dangled in front of him. Arie was on the floor, swallowing whatever gin was left in the bottle. There was a tall stool under the shuttered window, and he pulled it over to him, just below the noose.

"Look, Arie. Look at Daddy's present. It's a crown—no, a halo—for my angel. A red halo. Stand up, and come here to Daddy."

Arie gazed dully up at him. "Wha? Halo? Wha?"

"Here—Daddy will help you stand up." Kennedy reached for the woman, but she pulled away. He grasped her firmly under both arms, grateful that his gloves kept him from touching her flesh, and lifted her up. "That's right, Arie. Come to Daddy."

Arie could barely focus on the man and dropped the gin bottle on the floor, smashing it.

"Know what, Arie? Know what? This is more than a halo for my princess. It's a necklace—a beautiful red ruby necklace. It's a present, Arie. Let me help you put it on."

Arie looked at the broken pieces of glass from the gin bottle and paid no attention to the man placing the noose around her neck. "Broke—it's broke. Not me. Didn't do it. Not me. Don't get mad." She looked at the man. "Daddy?"

"Yes, Arie. It's your daddy. I'm not mad, Arie, you drunken little bitch. Here—let me help you stand up taller, like a big girl." Kennedy carefully lifted her up and, with some effort, balanced her precariously on the top edge of the stool. One hand held her while the other slipped the noose quickly over her head. Arie's attention was still on the broken pieces of glass at her feet. Holding her steady with one hand, he reached back to the other end of the rope and drew it taut against Arie's neck.

"Now, here comes the fun part, Arie. You know how Daddy likes games. You'll love this one." Kennedy released her, simultaneously pulling down hard on the rope with both hands. Arie choked and reached up to the noose. Kennedy had begun to sweat. He wrapped the rope several times around his hands.

"Good-bye, Arie," he said. "Now you and Daddy can be together forever." His right foot firmly kicked the stool out from under her. He watched her body swing back and forth for a time, fascinated by the surprised look on her face. Her legs kicked feebly. He marveled at the sounds she made and was pleased he had remembered to turn up the tape-recorder volume.

When he was certain she was dead, he lowered her to the floor. He straightened the stool, stepped up onto it, and tied the loose end of the rope firmly to the rafter, pulling on it with his full weight. Looking one final time at Arie's body, he left the bathroom, closed the door, and turned off the recorder. He placed it back in his briefcase and glanced quickly around the room. The broken glass on the floor was not a problem. He picked up his business card, put it in his pocket, and then paused at the box of Henry Clavin's medals. Should he take them or leave them? The photo of Clavin inside the box smiled up at him. *Why not leave them?* he thought. *How fitting. How appropriate.* There were no fingerprints, of course. Besides, no record of his fingerprints existed. There was no trace of his visit. He glanced once more at the bathroom door, smiled, and walked slowly out of the living room and the house.

Sitting in his car, Kennedy could scarcely contain his excitement. He pressed rewind on the recorder but knew it would not be safe to listen to it there outside the house. Trying to calm himself so that he could drive, he closed his eyes and breathed slowly, deeply. Then he started the car and drove slowly away from 57 Somerset Lane.

J ack sat across from Homes in his friend's Roswell PD office.

"So she says I ought to find some interesting case and keep my mind occupied."

Homes laughed. "So what's the payoff? If you solve some weird case, she goes to bed with you?"

"It doesn't always have to be about sex, Homes. The woman is trying to sooth my drunken soul."

"Well, a good romp in the sack might take care of that, too. Speaking of cases, I was going to bring this one home to you tonight." He threw a file across the desk to Jack. "This just came across the wire from Pendleton, South Carolina."

"Pendleton? Why would I care about some backwater town in South Carolina?" Jack opened the file and started reading.

"Oh, no reason. I just remembered you had an aunt or a cousin or an old girlfriend down there. I thought you might be interested."

"An aunt. Aunt Betty. Never kept up with her much. Nice old lady. Died maybe five years ago. What's the short version of this thing?" Jack waved the file at Homes.

"Well, it's real short. Came over the regional wire at the station yesterday. This woman, only about thirty-five, probably an alcoholic, hung herself. No reason they can figure out. Probably a suicide."

Jack smirked as he read. "How about alcoholism? That's reason enough."

"Hey, take it easy. I don't want you swingin' from my ceiling just because you want a beer!" Homes knew Jack enjoyed the back and forth about his drinking, and his reactions gave Homes a good measure of how Jack was handling his latest try at staying sober.

"Hey," Jack said, sitting up straight, looking at the file, "she lived on Somerset. Close to my aunt. I'm not sure, but Aunt Betty used to bring dinners to some woman down the street every once in a while. She worried about her eating regularly. Betty kind of adopted her. Could have been the suicide."

"Well, it ain't no big thing. The name of the town just caught my eye, and I remembered you had somebody down there."

"I'll take a look, but I guess I'm better off sticking to divorces and missing persons in Roswell and Alpharetta. There's enough of those to keep us both busy for the next twenty years. Besides, this is clearly a suicide."

"Could be. But you do get involved with some interesting women," Homes said.

"Yeah, sometimes. I told you I've sworn off women."

"My ass, you've sworn off. Who was that you went out with last weekend?"

"We're just friends," Jack said, smiling.

"Yeah, what do the teenagers call it—friends with benefits?"

Jack laughed. "The real benefit is that this woman isn't driving me to drink."

Homes smiled. "Yeah, I guess that is an advantage. Hey, Jack?"

"Yeah?"

"If you do get involved with some broad, try to keep your head this time!"

Jack winced at the reminder about a recent case in which some murderous Cambodian monks, out for revenge, had tried to decapitate him. That along with the woman he was involved with had set Jack off on a serious drunk. They still talked about it, and Jack could finally handle a little kidding.

"I'll try to keep that in mind, you bastard. And I'll take a look at this Pendleton thing just for the hell of it."

6.

About two weeks later, Jack found himself headed toward Pendleton, South Carolina, which was about two and a half hours northeast of Roswell and almost a straight shot on I-85. The town was actually a suburb of Clemson and only a short drive from the university. After calling ahead to the Anderson County sheriff's office, Jack made the drive in just over two hours, and with some time to kill, he drove by his aunt's old home on Somerset Lane. Whoever had bought it had kept the place up well, and it looked good. That was not the case with number 57, the site of the recent death. It was badly in need of repair. Several roof shingles were missing. A man was hammering a For Sale sign into the lawn. Even the sign could have used a coat of paint.

Jack found the sheriff's office on Camson Road, just a block or two outside the small town, and was greeted at the counter by a smiling, attractive brunette in a sharply pressed uniform. Her breasts were remarkable, and Jack figured they weren't real but wished he could find out. Still, he admired her for as long as he could without being obvious.

"Why, yes, Mr. Novak, Sheriff Calloway is expecting you. That's his office to the left. Go right in." Her smile followed him down the corridor.

Jack knocked and opened the door. Sheriff Calloway, who was sitting behind his cluttered desk, stood and offered his hand. He was a pleasant man in his early sixties, was a little overweight, and showed the easy assurance that many small-town officials displayed who had been in office for a long time. Jack noticed the plaques and various framed newspaper stories on the wall.

"Well, we don't get many city slickers like you down here in

Pendleton, Mr. Novak," the sheriff said, smiling. "What exactly is your interest in Arie Clavin?"

Preferring not to mention Homes and the private police information he had seen, Jack said, "I read about her death in the *Atlanta Constitution*, Sheriff, and the town name jumped out at me. My aunt lived down here for years—Betty Kimbrough—and—"

The sheriff interrupted. "Why, I knew ole Betty quite well. A fine lady. Always helping somebody out. We went to the same church."

"Yes, that was Aunt Betty all right. And I remembered that she used to take dinner to a younger woman down the street—she lived two doors down on Somerset. They'd play cards occasionally, I guess, and sometimes go to the movies. They were friends."

"Yup, sounds like Betty. Didn't know she was a friend of Arie's. But you know, Novak, that this really isn't what you'd call a formal *case*. I'm afraid Arie had been drinking quite a bit. Coroner said her blood-alcohol content was 0.22. I guess she was feelin' low and just decided to end it all. Never married, so no husband. No kids. No other family that we know of. She hung herself on a rafter in the bathroom. Now, *that* was weird."

"How so, Sheriff?"

"Well, that was where her father, Henry, killed himself all those years ago. And there was one other thing I thought was odd."

Jack waited.

"Henry's box of medals."

"Medals?"

The sheriff nodded. "Yep. Henry's medals from Vietnam. They were on the living-room table. Box was opened up, his picture inside. Like Arie had been lookin' at them. No prints on 'em, not even hers."

"What's unusual about the medals?"

"You'd have to know the family and the whole story, but Arie hated her father. The word around town was that he hurt the kid. Hurt the mother, too. Physically, I mean. He was drunk all the time. An all-round bad character. But that ain't all." The sheriff took a deep breath. "Clavin used to walk around town with them medals, showin' them and braggin' to anyone who would look, and then beggin' for money so's he could buy a drink."

"I guess that happens to a few vets from any war," Jack said, thinking of his own Gulf War service.

"Yeah, but here's the funny thing. Henry came up to me one day, askin' for a dollar. I gave it to him and asked him about the medals. He said he had pawned 'em. Pawned 'em someplace down in Columbia. He never told nobody exactly where. And his wife and Arie hated them things—hated everything about the man. They never woulda gone after them medals. Especially with that picture inside. So where'd they come from?" The sheriff stared at Jack for a long time.

"That is pretty curious, Sheriff. Did Arie go out of town much?"

"Dang near never. Didn't have no car."

Jack considered this for a moment. "Any history of threatening suicide?"

"Nope. Not that we ever heard. And we interviewed the folks she worked with out at the home. That's the Evergreen Home on Blanchard, across from the Methodist Church. They liked her well enough, said she never complained. They knew she drank some, but not while she was working. They was about the only friends she had. Two of those folks found her."

"And she didn't leave a note?"

"Nope. Nothin' like that. Nobody in the neighborhood saw anything. The whole thing was probly a little odd, but there wasn't enough to sink our teeth into."

"Sure sounds like it, Sheriff. I thought I'd check it out because of her friendship with my aunt, but I'm not trying to stir anything up." Jack knew that small-town law enforcement didn't like outsiders meddling in their cases or trying to show them up.

"Didn't think you were, Novak. I had Aubrey out there on the desk put this here file together for you. It's everything we got on the death, some photos, description of the place, and notes about talking to a few of her friends." He handed it to Jack.

"That's awfully nice of you, Sheriff. Thank you. If I'm out of line, please tell me. Is there any chance I could see those medals if you still have them?"

The sheriff scratched his jaw and thought for a moment. "Well, I still got 'em down in the evidence room. The case—if it ever was a case—is completely closed and off the books. How about if I loan 'em to you while you're checking into things? Long as you bring 'em back. Tell you what. If you're stayin' over tonight, I'll have Aubrey bring 'em out to you. Best place to stay in town is the Get-A-Way Motel."

"That would be great, Sheriff. Sounds like the medals are the only clue we have."

The sheriff scratched his head. "Maybe, but a clue to what? Tell you what, Novak. There's nothing on my schedule right now. If you've got the time, I'll take you out to the house, and you can look around inside if you like. Afterward, I can take you to lunch."

"That would be very helpful, Sheriff. Thanks again. And it would be my pleasure to take you to lunch."

7.

T he two men pushed their plates away and sipped sweet iced tea. The sheriff broke the silence.

"So did you get anything out of walking around the house, Novak?"

"Not much. You say nothing has been moved or changed?"

"Nothing at all. We had tape around the house for a while. Just started to board it up some. The bank that owns the place doesn't want to put any money into it to fix it up. It may never sell."

"The rope that Arie hung herself with—anything unusual about it? Maybe the knots in it?"

"Well, I don't know much about knots, son, but they looked normal to me. You got photos of 'em in that there file we gave you."

"Sheriff, you think of everything. I may just be wasting my time, but would you mind if I drove around the area and talked to some people in the neighborhood? They may have seen or heard something."

"Not a bit, son. We talked to most of the folks on the street, like I said. But suit yourself. If anyone gives you any problems, you just tell 'em that Joe Dan Calloway said it was okay." He handed Jack his card.

"Thanks again, Sheriff. Looks like I'll stay over and head back to Atlanta in the morning."

Jack knocked on the doors of two houses close by Arie Clavin's and got nowhere with the residents—an old man in one and a woman with a child in the other. Neither had seen or heard anything the morning the body was found.

The third home Jack chose was three doors down from the Clavin place. An elderly woman answered the door.

"Excuse me, ma'am. My name is Jack Novak. I'm a detective from Atlanta looking into the Arie Clavin, ah, death. I'm Betty Kimbrough's nephew, and they were friends." He handed her the sheriff's card. "Sheriff Calloway has given me permission to ask Arie Clavin's neighbors a few questions."

Eyeing Jack carefully, the woman nodded slowly. "I guess that would be okay. I knew Betty. Miss her. My name is Amy Stroker. Now, what about Arie?"

"Thank you, ma'am. I wonder if you saw anyone, perhaps a stranger, around Arie's home the day she was—the day she died?"

"Why, no. I told the sheriff. No one on the street that I saw."

Jack nodded. "Anything unusual happen that day? Anything at all?"

She shook her head. "Nothing. No, nothing."

"Thanks for your help, Mrs. Stroker. Sorry to have bothered you."

"No bother, young man." She smiled and closed the door.

As Jack turned and walked down the stairs in front of the house, he saw an older black man with a rake in his hands watching him. Jack walked over to him and smiled.

"Good afternoon. My name is Jack Novak, a private detective from—"

"I was listening to you talk to Miss Stroker. I heard you."

"Then you know the sheriff said I—"

"I heard that, too." The man moved the rake around nervously. "I do a little yard work for Miss Stroker. Been working for her for over thirty year. Used to help Miss Clavin, too. Did it for nothing. I liked her."

"Glad to hear that, Mr.—uh—"

"You ain't gonna get me in trouble talking to you, is you? The name is Harold. Just Harold."

"Not at all, Harold. I'm trying to find out if a neighbor saw anything or anyone unusual that day."

Harold moved the rake around again. "I seen something. Someone."

Jack waited.

"I seen a man when I was coming around the side o' Miss Stroker's house that morning. Been trimming them *Melia* trees in back. He was walkin' up toward Miss Clavin's house and didn't see me. He park his car all the ways down here, not in front o' Miss Clavin's house. White people act funny sometimes."

"Did you know him?"

Harold shook his head. "Not from around here. Don't live here. I know most folks around here. Looked like a rich white man to me. Nice suit. Nice briefcase."

"What did he do?"

"He walk up to Miss Clavin's house and knock on the door. She come in a while."

"Could you hear him—hear what they were talking about?"

"No. I figure he was sellin' something, and I had work to do, so I went back in the backyard."

Jack thought for a moment. "This is very helpful, Harold. Did you notice anything unusual about the car?"

"Nope. It was new and black. It had one o' them rental signs on the front bumper."

"Did you see him go inside the house? Or hear anything?"

"I done already tole you. I went around back here." He waved the rake toward the rear of the house. "That's all I know." He turned to walk away.

"Thanks very much, Harold," Jack said to the man's back.

Thinking there was probably nothing to what Harold saw, Jack got into his car and made some quick notes. He was tired and looked forward to getting some rest. "Checking the rental thing may be worth the time," he said to himself. He drove down to a local coffee shop that offered free Wi-Fi and brought his notebook computer inside. After ordering a large dark blend with a fancy name, he sat down at one of the tables and went to work. There were only three car-rental companies in Pendleton, none of them a nationally known business, and he wrote down the address for each of them. They were all located out by the small local airport, which was a quick ten-minute drive.

He had no luck at his first stop and headed down the street to the next business.

An elderly man with bright blue eyes, wearing a faded gray shirt, was sitting behind the counter. The man smiled at Novak. "I was goin' to guess you needed a car, but I seen you drive up in one. Guess I'm wrong."

Jack grinned at him. "No, I don't need a car, but I do need some information. Maybe you can help me out."

"Well, I ain't exactly covered up with business, young fella. What's on your mind?"

Jack went through his explanation and showed the man the sheriff's card.

"If Joe Dan says you're okay, that's good enough for me. What do you want to know?"

"I'm Betty Kimbrough's nephew, and I'm down here checking out a few things about the day her neighbor, Arie Clavin, died. Can you tell me if anyone rented a car from you on or around May fifth of this year? I don't have much information. Probably a late model. Black. Might have been a well-dressed man. Sorry I don't have more."

The man laughed. "Son, that's about all you need. I only got five cars, and they're all black and no more than three years old. Low mileage. Nobody that comes to Pendleton drives very far." He reached back to a large box. "May fifth, you say?"

"Yes. Might be a day or two before or after."

"Well, May fifth was a Tuesday, and I'm closed on Sunday. So are the other two rentals. I can check on May fourth and fifth and maybe the sixth." He looked up quizzically at Jack.

"That would be fine. I hope I'm not putting you to much trouble."

"Like I say, son, on a slow day like this, it gives me somethin' to do."

The man flipped through some cards in the file box, pausing to check dates, and finally pulled one out. "Now, this here man I remember. Kinda tall, well dressed, like you said. I recollect he drove up here in a taxi from our airport. The thing I remember most—he was smilin' funny."

"How do you mean?"

"It was kinda like he didn't really mean it—the smile. Just makin' believe with it, if you know what I mean." The man pushed the file card across to Jack. "I recollect he said he was a lawyer. Probably why he smiled funny. A lot a them lawyers do that."

Jack laughed and wrote down the name on the card: Thomas Kennedy of Olden, Stormwell, and Kennedy in Atlanta. Jack worked with a lot of law firms all over Atlanta and had never heard of this one, but that didn't necessarily mean anything.

"Do you have a credit-card receipt?"

"Nope. He paid cash. Not many people do that anymore, ya know?"

"Is this his driver's license number on the card?"

"Yup. Georgia license. Looked good. You think he was up to something?"

Jack shook his head. "Not really. Can't tell for sure. This was the only lead I had, and it may not mean anything at all. You didn't, by any chance, make a copy of the license?"

The man laughed. "Son, that's a little fancy for us in Pendleton. Sorry. I hope you find what yer lookin' for. Wish I could be more help."

Jack thought for a moment. "Maybe you can. The sheriff told me about a motel close by and maybe a restaurant."

"Why, sure. The local joke is that the motel ain't clean, but it's close. Motel about a half mile to your left as you pull out of my place. They can tell you about the restaurant. Don't expect much, now."

"You've helped quite a bit, Mr.—"

"Bill Calloway, son. I'm the sheriff's brother."

Jack found the Get-A-Way Motel quickly and repeated his questions. The clerk, who was also the owner, found the room registration easily. The clerk reported a room registered to a man of the same name and address: Thomas Kennedy, Atlanta, Georgia.

"Only remember one funny thing about the man."

"What was that?"

"His bed was tore up."

"How do you mean?"

"It was stripped. Sheets and pillowcases both. The cleaning girl raised hell about it to me. Said it took her extra time to put it all back together."

"Sounds a little odd, doesn't it?"

The man agreed.

"Oh, and I'll need a room for tonight—just a single."

"All our rooms are queens. That okay?"

"Sure," Jack said. "I'll sleep like a king."

The small restaurant two blocks from the motel was called Lucy's Lunch Box. Lucy had no records that amounted to anything and said there were no credit-card receipts for May 5 or 6. Most of her customers paid cash, she said. Jack had hit another dead end.

Back in his car, Jack called Homes in his office. "Sorry to wake you up, Detective Kinney."

"You still down in Pendleton?"

"Yeah, and I need you to check on something for me."

"Are you asking me to use the private facilities of the Roswell police force to assist you in one of your personal cases, Mr. Novak?"

Jack chuckled. "No more than usual, you old bastard. Homes, check a law firm for me, will you? Olden, Stormwell, and Kennedy in Atlanta— but they could be anywhere close by. Name is Thomas Kennedy." Jack could hear Homes's computer keys clicking.

"That firm isn't ringing a bell, Jack. Nothing showing up in the state databases for law firms either. What name did you say?"

"Thomas Kennedy, and I've got a Georgia driver's license number." He gave the numbers slowly to Homes and then heard more clicking.

"Nope. There is no current or past driver's license with that number, Jack. I've got—let's see—seven Thomas Kennedys in the database. Three of them are deceased. None of them associated with a law firm in the area."

Homes did some more typing. "Jack, there's not a law firm in the country with that name."

"You sure?"

"Am I ever wrong?"

"Often." Jack laughed. "Maybe I've got something, Homes. Maybe not. Think I'll stay over and check on a few things. If you find anything else, save it for me."

"Right. See you back in Atlanta in the morning."

It had been a busy day. Just as Jack was thinking about turning in for the night, there was a slight rap at his door. He opened it to find Aubrey, the young woman who had greeted him at the sheriff's office that morning, her uniform as crisp and fresh as it had been hours ago.

"Hi," she said, smiling at him. "The sheriff asked me to drop this off for you." She handed him the box of medals. "My name is—"

Jack smiled at her. "Your name is Aubrey, and thanks for the box."

"I didn't think you'd remember," she said, looking around the small motel room and then walking inside.

"Men don't usually forget your name, do they?"

They both laughed. "Not so far," she said.

"I don't have anything here to offer you," Jack said. "My hospitality is pretty thin."

"That's all right," she said, choosing to sit on his bed rather than in one of the chairs. "I looked you up on the Internet."

"Really," he said, sitting in a chair across from her. "And what did you find?"

"Not much more than I already knew. That you were a detective from Roswell, Georgia, and a former cop in the same town." She eased back on the bed slightly, relaxing on her elbows. "You're single, and you were in one of the Gulf Wars, too."

"Probably before you were born," Jack said, smiling.

"I'm really not that young," she said.

Jack nodded. "And what about you? All I know is Aubrey."

She stretched out on the bed, facing him. "Aubrey Sanders. I'm twenty-five, lived here all my life, lost my virginity when I was a junior in high school. I have a master's degree in criminology, and I'm a sworn officer, not just a clerk. Oh, and I'm single, too."

Jack looked surprised. "A master's degree? Then what—"

"What am I doing in Pendleton, sitting in the sheriff's office?"

"I wasn't going to say—"

She grinned and kicked off her shoes. "That's okay. I'm here because I want to be. My family is here. Uncle Joe Dan will retire in a couple of years, and I intend to run for sheriff. I'd be one of the few female sheriffs in South Carolina."

"So the sheriff is your uncle," Jack said. "Is everyone in this town related to everyone else?"

"Pretty close," Aubrey said as she got up from the bed and walked toward him, stopping in front of his chair. "One other thing."

"What's that?"

"I'm not the shy, retiring type," she said, moving smoothly onto his lap, putting her arms around his neck, and kissing him—softly at first and then more intensely.

Jack was surprised and then responded to her, moving his hands around her soft body, his mouth on hers and then on her neck, her chest, and her mouth once again. Aubrey groaned, pulled off her trousers, positioned herself on top of his growing hardness, and began to rock back and forth. His hands went to her ass and helped to position her. Her movements grew firmer and stronger until she climaxed.

"I've wanted to do that with you all day," she said. "And I know it didn't do you much good with your pants on, so let's see if your bed works." Aubrey slid off his lap, took his hand, and walked slowly to the bed. Her other hand began to unbutton her blouse. Jack had already released the belt on his pants and was starting on his shirt.

Aubrey turned the covers back and laughed as Jack tried to pull his shoes off without untying them. "In a hurry, Detective?" she said. "Can I help?"

"You can help with a lot of things, but I can handle the shoes," he said, reaching for her.

She had a remarkable body, and Jack let his eyes and then his mouth move over it slowly, occasionally using his tongue on her breasts. No doubt, they were real. Aubrey groaned again and pulled him on top of her, reaching down and moving him inside her.

"Take your time, Detective," she said. "We've got all night."

"I'll take my time later. You've got me too excited right now, Officer. Women in uniform have always turned me on." They both smiled as they clung to each other.

"I guess I've heard that a few times before," she said.

Jack hadn't had a night like this in over a year, since a rocky relationship with a woman in Roswell. But that night had been fueled by drugs and alcohol. With Aubrey, it was just mutual desire and appreciation for their bodies.

While they were resting, Jack kissed her and said, "Aubrey, tell me how you got your name."

"From my mother. From some song she liked in the seventies when she was a kid. I was born in eighty-nine. She had me late. She would walk around our apartment holding me, singing the song. All I can remember is the first line: 'And Aubrey was her name.'"

"Bread," Jack said. "Bread was the group that had a big hit with it."

"How do you know that?" Aubrey said. "You're the first person I've met who has ever heard of Bread."

"The music was around the house when I was growing up, too. I'm also a Bobby Darin fan."

"Who?"

"Another singer popular in the sixties and seventies. It's not important."

"It's important that you know about him. And Bread. At least, it's important to me."

She moved on top of him, and they began again.

Jack loved the feel of her, and he explored every part of her body. He sighed and looked at her. "Aubrey, tell me why the boys around here haven't scooped you up by now."

Aubrey snuggled her breasts into Jack's chest. "Well, I have been scooped from time to time, in a manner of speaking, but nothing serious. I want more out of life than being a farmer's wife, and that's primarily what happens when you get married in Pendleton. Nothing wrong with it; I just want something else. And I've been told a time or two that I'm too aggressive for a girl."

Jack had to laugh at that. "Well, you'll never hear that from me tonight, lady."

"That's good," Aubrey said, "because I'm ready to try a country thing or two on you, Detective."

"I'm always open to new experiences," Jack said, admiring the way she used her hands and then her mouth.

A few hours later, Aubrey stirred and shook Jack. "I've got to go now. I'm supposed to open the office at eight, and I need to take a shower."

"You smell fine to me," Jack said. "I hate to have you leave, but it will give me time to recuperate. And I don't want the sheriff mad at me."

Aubrey got out of bed and started pulling on her clothes. "Jack, tell me something."

"Sure. Anything."

"What's wrong with you?"

"What? What do you mean?"

She sat on the edge of the bed and reached for his hand. "You seem like such a nice guy. You've got a regular job. Great sense of humor. You're terrific in bed. So what's your problem?"

"Do I have to have a problem?" Jack said, smiling.

"Maybe I'm just used to the men around here. There are a lot of problems in a small town. I'd like to see you again, and I just want to know what I'm getting into."

Jack nodded. "I can understand that." He thought for a moment about how much to tell her. "Aubrey, I've got a problem with alcohol. I'm dealing with it. I'm in a program, seeing a doctor, going to meetings. But it's a serious problem. I'm an alcoholic."

"Thanks for being honest with me," she said. "I deal with drunks a lot in my job. You don't seem like one."

"I appreciate you saying that. But the fact is, I am one. It's been almost a year now since my last drink, and I'm feeling a lot better. I have good friends who are helping, too. But the problem is there, and it always will be."

Aubrey smiled at him and patted his hand. "So when will I see you again?" she asked, starting to get dressed again.

"I have the feeling I'll be making several trips to Pendleton in the near future. You'll have to be looking for new evidence for me."

Aubrey smiled. "I'll do the best I can."

"Oh, and, Aubrey?"

"Yes?"

"The second line of your song—'A not-so-ordinary girl or name'—suits you perfectly." He leaned over and kissed her.

9.

"**T**rouble is, Homes, there was nothing in the house. Nothing except a box of old Vietnam medals from the woman's father's service. The sheriff couldn't find any prints but hers. The Clavin woman was known to drink a lot, and her blood alcohol was off the charts. She hung herself in the same bathroom where her father did the deed thirty or thirty-five years ago."

Homes took another swig of beer. "I've got to stop buying this shit."

Jack looked up. "What's that?"

"This goddamned fancy beer. I can't pronounce the name of it, and it tastes so damned sour I think it's spoiled. But they all taste that way nowadays. What the hell ever happened to PBR?"

Jack laughed. "You lead a tough life, Homes. Spoiled beer. And you can still buy Pabst anywhere. They drink a hell of a lot of it up in Athens at UGA."

"Yeah, but it don't taste like much either." He looked thoughtful, flipping through the Arie Clavin file. "So you think this guy Kennedy—you think that ain't his real name?"

"Could be. But it may not even be the same guy Harold the yardman saw walking up to the Clavin house. He never saw him go inside anyway."

Homes nodded. "One thing we know for sure: his license was bogus. I had the bureau run a deep check on him, and the license number doesn't exist either. Not in Atlanta, not anywhere. And I ran the law firm's name through Martindale again. There's no such firm. Never has been."

"So what do you think?"

"I think you got something going, Jack, my boy."

"Yeah, but what? And where do I go from here?"

"Well, from the look of you, my guess is that you'll be headin' back to Pendleton pretty soon. I haven't seen you look this whipped since you were dating Roxanne Rhoden."

"I'll have you know I was in an all-night meeting with local law enforcement," Jack said, trying to keep a straight face. He picked up the box of medals, looked them over, and then handed them to Homes. "This whole so-called suicide is strange. And this thing with the medals is fuckin' weird too."

10.

K ill Devil Hills, North Carolina, a small town of about six thousand, sat squarely on the Atlantic Ocean, just south of Kitty Hawk and the Wright Brothers National Monument and north of Nags Head on the Outer Banks. Although difficult to reach, it was a popular summer spot and a typical beach community. During the winter, the population dropped to about 2,500 die-hard beach folk. There were a few small seafood restaurants, motels, and scattered businesses. One could rent a boat for deep-sea fishing. A few residents sold beach jewelry from their homes, shells and glass bits they'd found along the beach.

The Hills had been hit by hurricanes and many other strong storms several times in recent years, which had limited the number of year-round residents. There had been a few lovely summer homes along the coast, but most of them had been destroyed by the storms. Only two minor highways connected the Hills with the main coast. For most of the year, it was a perfect hideaway.

The man who had called himself Thomas Kennedy in Pendleton, South Carolina, was finally back home—his real home. He owned several houses in five states, but he felt most comfortable in the Hills. He had selected the small town both for its unique name—a good omen— and for its remoteness, especially in the colder months. It was only an hour and a half's drive directly north to a fairly large airport in Norfolk, Virginia. From there, he could be anywhere in a matter of hours.

Kennedy's small, weather-beaten house was almost a mile from his nearest neighbor and attracted no attention. There were excellent beaches in Kill Devil, but Kennedy had selected his home just north of the town, where the beachfront began to disappear. Bathers and campers seldom came close to his home.

No one knew his real name. He seldom thought of it himself. A faded sign outside the house offered beach jewelry for sale, but it was only a facade. Kennedy had bought out a beachcomber's small stock of shells and glass but did not actively work the business. The one thing he enjoyed about the ruse was the name he had chosen for the shop: the Devil's Smile.

While his home was small and simply furnished, Kennedy had not skimped on expensive communications equipment. He had powerful satellite radio, television, and Internet connections, all carefully concealed. The equipment had been installed by a bright young man from Elizabeth City who, unfortunately, had asked too many questions and had mysteriously disappeared soon after he'd completed his work for Kennedy. The local sheriff's brief investigation had turned up nothing.

When a powerful storm threatened the Hills, Kennedy and other residents would simply move inland, perhaps to Elizabeth City, Edenton, or another small community, until the danger passed. Kennedy paid his taxes and other bills promptly. He was a model citizen in all respects.

Kennedy had just finished listening to his recording of his visit to Arie Clavin for the seventh time. There was always some nuance in her sounds of terror that he had missed before. It was like reliving the whole event again. Smiling, Kennedy began reading the *Norfolk Pilot-Star*. The newspaper had been experiencing the same extreme slump in business that had affected most newspapers over the past few years, but he still found its regional coverage of the South to be interesting and helpful as he selected stories that caught his eye. To supplement the *Pilot-Star*, he had Sunday editions of the Raleigh *News and Observer* and the *Atlanta Journal-Constitution* mailed to him. It was the Atlanta daily he picked up now, turning to the local section.

He always found the local news to be most helpful. He read it slowly and carefully, looking for the sorrowful human-interest stories that seemed to attract most readers. A careless grandmother allowed her grandson to electrocute himself when he pulled a space heater into the bathtub. A father backed his car over his unseen child, crushing her body. A teenager accidentally discharged a gun while showing it to his five-year-old brother, killing him instantly. He looked for stories that—what was the phrase?—tugged at one's heart. Kennedy had never experienced that feeling. Truthfully, he had never experienced any heartfelt feeling. But he knew that these incidents made other people emotionally vulnerable, and that was what he was looking for—what he wanted and needed. Through the victims' stories, he could share their most extreme feelings—their terror, dread, regret. And when he visited them, if they needed some assistance in recalling the moments when their terror was most heightened, he could provide that help. And by helping them, he helped himself control the gnawing, growing hunger he felt. Drugs, alcohol, physical pain—he knew how to use them all to bring about the result he needed.

He had received two new files to review from his current private investigator. He never used the same PI twice, and they were always chosen from cities far from the ones he selected for his work. He would send the investigators brief information culled from newspaper stories or obituaries and ask for thorough background information on the lives and personal habits of his prospects. Using the investigative reports, he'd be ready for another trip soon. What was that other clichéd saying—'Idle hands are the devil's workshop'? Another good omen when one lived in Kill Devil Hills. Neither of the two files was impressive, but they were all he had at the moment. He chose the one labeled "Carson Weber from Birmingham" and began to read.

11.

"I don't need to have wine with dinner, Jack." Laura placed her purse on the empty chair at their table.

"I know that, Laura. It doesn't bother me. But as my former psychiatrist, you should know that already." They both smiled and picked up the menus. They had agreed that Greenwoods on Green Street in Roswell was their favorite restaurant and a good spot to begin their nonprofessional relationship. It was nice but not too nice and was cozy but not romantic. And the food was great.

Laura ordered the duck with plum sauce. Jack ordered shrimp and grits. He would have preferred the southern fried chicken, but not knowing what might happen between them for the rest of the evening, he thought that being relatively greaseless might be a good idea. The fact that Laura was unconcerned was another reason he liked her.

"So tell me what you've been doing lately—this case you've been working on." She paused as her glass of red wine was brought to the table.

Jack thought for a moment. "Well, I really can't call it a case—at least not yet." He explained about his trip to Pendleton and the inquiries he had made about the death of Arie Clavin. He told her that he and Homes agreed that something didn't feel right about the man with the phony driver's license but admitted it might just be their suspicious natures.

Laura laughed. "Well, I don't have a suspicious nature, and it sounds odd to me. Especially those two men at the rental-car place and the motel mentioning the man's strange smile and torn-up bed."

"Leave it to a psychiatrist to latch on to that," Jack said, smiling. "Remind me not to smile at you that way."

Laura nodded. "That's just it, Jack. Most people smile sincerely—or at least in an unguarded way. Two unsophisticated men from this small South Carolina town thought his smile was somehow out of place."

"I agree. It doesn't feel right. But where do I go from here? Do I drive around looking for people with funny smiles or ask to check strangers' driver's licenses? I don't know how to move this along."

Their food arrived, and they ate in silence for a while. "Any mysteries in your own life, Laura? What's been keeping you busy?"

"I can't talk about my patients, of course. Besides, you were my most interesting patient, but now you're—"

"What? A civilian of sorts?"

Laura laughed. "A civilian. I like that description. Better than 'former patient.'" Laura grew quiet for a moment. "The only thing in my life that's troubling is my father's illness. I think I've mentioned it before."

Jack nodded. "Yes, I think you said it was Alzheimer's and getting progressively worse."

"That's right. Dad was an attorney—and a good one. I guess that's why it's twice as troubling to see his mind slowly drifting away. Sometimes he's still so sharp. But those times are getting more infrequent." She paused and took a deep breath. "And now he's experiencing a lot of pain. It's cancer, and it's bad."

"It's a good thing he's in your same apartment complex so you can keep an eye on him."

"Yes, and I've got nursing help to stay with him, at least for now." Laura stopped eating, and Jack could see tears forming in her eyes. "Last week, he ..."

"What is it?" He reached for her hand.

"Oh, nothing unexpected, really. Last week, he made me promise that if he got worse, if he lost it completely, I'd, well, do something to help him."

"Euthanasia," Jack said softly.

Laura nodded. "Yes. I've always been morally opposed to that, but when it's your own parent and you see them slipping away ..." Her voice drifted off.

"That's a tough call all right. I don't know what I'd do in the same situation. I just wouldn't want a parent to suffer. Anyone I was close to, really."

Laura took a deep breath and finished her wine. "I'm sure it will work out. Let's talk about something else."

They finished dinner with small talk and left the restaurant. Jack realized he had no idea how to approach the rest of the evening. He wanted to go somewhere private with Laura to see how their relationship might progress. On the other hand, he still thought of her as his psychiatrist, even though she had found him another doctor.

"Jack, I'd like to continue our talk tonight, and I want to invite you to my place. I'd also like you to know that I'm not ready for anything beyond talking right now. Is that okay, or do you think I'm being old-fashioned?"

He smiled at her and shook his head. "Not a bit. In fact, you've solved a problem I had with deciding where to go and what to do. That all sounds good to me."

They spent the rest of the evening in her apartment, talking about how they'd both grown up, where they had gone to school, and what they had done as they'd started their professional lives. Laura already knew a great deal about Jack's past but listened intently to the story of his recent murder case involving stolen jewels and Cambodian monks who were out to kill him.

"Jack, why are you smiling? My God, you were almost, well, decapitated."

"I'm smiling because those lovely brown eyes of yours kept getting bigger as I was telling you the details. Homes calls me the Headless Horse's Ass."

They both smiled. "I'd like to meet Homes. You talk about him all the time, and he's obviously a key element in your life."

Jack threw his head back and laughed. "A key element—I've got to remember to call him that when I get back to our place. I've called him a lot of other less-attractive names."

"I'll bet you have. And I'm sorry I started to sound like a doctor again."

"Not at all. I like that about you. I like a lot of things about you."

They looked at each other and realized this was the moment that happened at the beginning of every relationship—when they had a decision to make. Would things turn romantic, or would they remain just friends?

"Laura, I heard what you said when we left the restaurant, and this is probably a good time for me to say good night and head for the apartment. Homes always has some good tales to tell when he gets back from a date."

Before he could stand up, Laura leaned toward him and kissed him lightly but nicely. "Thanks, Jack. You can always exaggerate about your own date." They laughed as they stood up and headed for Laura's front door.

"I'm so used to making an appointment to see you again. How should we handle that now?"

"I'll let you decide some clever way," Laura said. "After all, you're the detective."

12.

"**S**o this time, I'm Gregory Stone," the man said aloud. "Mr. Stone is an insurance investigator from Memphis." Smiling, he looked at the new driver's license and business card in his wallet and opened the manila file.

"Carson Weber," he said to himself. Mr. Weber, sixty-seven, was a widower living on the outskirts of Birmingham, Alabama. Carelessly, Mr. Weber had allowed his granddaughter, Sharon, age two, to drown in his pool while he was caring for her. He continued to grieve, of course. Most people would. Mr. Weber's wife had passed away. Baby Sharon's parents no longer communicated with Mr. Weber, according to the file. Neither did his neighbors. Mr. Weber was, tragically, miserably alone. A newspaper story and obituary had given Mr. Stone the distraught grandfather's location.

Stone sighed contentedly. A dead baby, a grieving old man, and a swimming pool—all the tools he needed. But as he continued to read, he became more and more disappointed.

His new project, Carson Weber, apparently had few vices. Looking over the detailed report, Stone found no history of Weber drinking or taking other drugs. He was not even a smoker. He was simply careless, and his carelessness had caused the drowning of his two-year-old granddaughter, Sharon. Stone had been in this predicament before and found the results unsatisfactory. People without vices were not as susceptible as Arie Clavin had been in Pendleton and often did not respond well to his manipulations. Furthermore, the child, Sharon, had died three years before, which was another possible difficulty. Time could either help or hurt. Nevertheless, he was prepared to deal with the problem. Besides, Stone was growing restless, and Weber was his best opportunity for the moment.

Mr. Stone had become adept in the use of several neuromuscular drugs in his work. Generic versions were easily obtained on the Internet, primarily from China and Thailand, and required no refrigeration. The drugs, often referred to as "blocking drugs," were frequently used during medical operations, along with anesthesia, to temporarily paralyze patients and allow the doctors to operate without premature muscular reactions. Blocking drugs were similar to a derivative called Rohypnol, popularly known in pill form as a date-rape drug, or *roofie*. Stone was repulsed by the idea of having sexual contact with another human being under any circumstances. But the idea of performing those disgusting acts with a paralyzed victim was especially repugnant. Had people lost all sense of morality? Stone often imagined himself a doctor—at least a medical prodigy—because of his skills learned in using these drugs. True, these skills had been developed through trial and error, and several of his patients had not survived—none of them had survived, in fact. But he had learned well.

Because these drugs often paralyzed breathing in his victims and ended their lives too soon to record their last terrifying moments, Stone's experiments had developed drug derivatives that would allow the individuals to continue breathing for a time. He had nicknamed his favorite drug blend Neuromaxim. Most important, his blended drugs, odorless and tasteless, also permitted his victims to continue to feel the physical and emotional pain he inflicted, despite their paralysis. With proper dosages, they could usually make no sounds. In less than an hour, all traces of the drug disappeared completely. Stone often reflected that modern medical science was wonderful. Of course, the use of these drugs did not allow him to experience the full range of outcries and pleadings from his victims. He had learned to satisfy himself temporarily with the looks of horror on his silent prey. They were carefully recorded with his cell phone and later transferred to computer discs.

How about meeting me halfway—say, in Greenville? That will give us more time."

Jack and Aubrey had met there once before, and their relationship was growing.

"That sounds good," she said. "There's a Comfort Inn on the outskirts of town."

Jack laughed. "You sound pretty familiar with that one."

Aubrey chuckled too. "I told you I make my own choices."

"I want you to know I'm a big spender," Jack said. "How about the Motel 6 on the other side of town?"

"Now who's showing off?" she said.

"Just good detective work. Seriously, there's a pretty nice Hyatt Regency downtown that will keep us close to the McAlister Auditorium. Maybe we can take in a show."

"The Hyatt is fine," she said. "But what makes you think I'll let you out of the room?"

Jack laughed again. "Exactly what I was thinking about you. Why don't we get together late afternoon Friday—say, about four o'clock?"

"That's perfect. You may not recognize me without my uniform."

"I don't think that will be a problem. See you soon."

Jack arrived at the Hyatt at about three o'clock, showered, and lay down on the bed to reread all the information he and Homes had put together about the character they had started to call Mr. Nobody. He admitted to himself that they only had bits and pieces, but their cop senses told them that there was a lot more to the situation. The knock on the door brought him out of detective mode quickly, and he smiled as he walked over and asked who it was.

"This is Officer Aubrey Sanders. I understand you have an underage woman in your room, and I'm here to put you in hand cuffs."

As Jack opened the door, Aubrey stepped into his arms, and they wrapped themselves around each other. Not wanting the kiss to end, Jack kicked the door closed. Then he paused for a minute to look at Aubrey.

"You don't look like an officer of the law without your uniform, but I hope you brought the hand cuffs with you."

Aubrey massaged her body into his. "I brought everything with me."

"I can see that. And feel it." They kissed again.

"Nice touch, you being in your underwear. Looks like you're eager to see me," Aubrey said, glancing at his hardness.

"In this case, looks are not deceiving," Jack said. "I was also catching up on some detective work. I work better the fewer clothes I wear."

"We'll see about that," she said, unzipping her skirt and pulling her blouse over her head. She wasn't wearing a bra and, as usual, wore no underwear. "Want me to take a shower?"

"Maybe tomorrow," Jack said, dropping his shorts. "I want to smell you and taste you just the way you are."

They walked together to the king-sized bed and fell onto it simultaneously. Then moans, shouts, and sighs filled the room.

"Have I ever told you how incredible you are?" Jack said.

"Several times. But don't stop." Aubrey moved on top of him. "You said you didn't mind this."

"I don't mind anything about you, and I especially like this," he said, moving his mouth over her breasts. Aubrey moved slowly at first and then more quickly, drawing him deeply inside her. He studied the look on her face as she climaxed, and then he kissed her softly.

"Stay right where you are," he said. "I want to feel you." He massaged her back slowly as they kissed.

"This is only going to get you in more trouble, Detective," she said. "How about if we switch positions?"

"I thought you'd never ask," Jack said.

They woke up about an hour later. Jack admired her body as she turned to him.

"I can put my clothes back on," she said, smiling.

"Don't even try," he said.

"How about mixing business with pleasure? Bring me up to date on your case."

Jack had been telling Aubrey about his search for the man they had nicknamed Mr. Nobody, and he quickly added the little new information he and Homes had developed. Aubrey nodded as he spoke, occasionally asking questions that told Jack she had been following their work closely.

"Jack, I went back over to Arie Clavin's house and did a slow walk-through. Just as you said, there was nothing at all. I felt the same thing you did when you visited the home. I couldn't prove anything, but it just didn't feel right."

"Yeah. There are just too many small things hanging, and they bother Homes and me. Trouble is, we still don't know where to go from here. This guy is too clever and careful to be a first-timer."

Aubrey nodded. "I think the same thing, but I remember a criminology class at Clemson wherein we spent two weeks studying unsolved murders over the past century. In almost every case, they never identified the killer. Most of the time, there were either no prints at all, or the prints turned up a zero even when we created modern databases."

"That's another thing that bugs me," Jack said. "How many other murderers are out there right now that will never be caught because they leave no trail and we just can't identify them?"

"My instructor, who used to be a cop, said that statistically, there had to be hundreds. Maybe half of those were one-time killers who never tried it again. The rest are like this guy—this Kennedy guy or whatever his real name is. They go on killing for as long as they want. And they always want more."

"I've told you about my former psychiatrist, Laura Benjamin, who suggested that keeping my mind focused on a difficult case would probably help my drinking problem more than anything else. Well, it's working."

Aubrey turned away for a moment. "Jack, you told me you had been dating her." She rolled back over to face him. "Are you in love with her?"

Jack had known this moment with Aubrey would come. "No. We're close, and we like each other. But there's never been any talk about love. When she was my shrink, she and I agreed that I have a problem with loving someone. She said it was because I don't think I'm good enough to love anyone, but I don't know where that came from in my life."

Neither one of them said anything for a while. "Jack, you know you don't have a problem with me on the subject of love, don't you?"

"I know."

"I wasn't looking for that when we started seeing each other, and I'm still not expecting it. But you ought to know that you are good enough—good enough to love someone and to be loved by that person. I may be young, but I think I'm a pretty fair judge."

"I don't know what to say to that. I've still got a long way to go."

"Don't worry about it," she said, reaching for him. "Maybe I can do something to distract you."

14.

J ack didn't wake up right away to the persistent phone ringing. In his dream, he was back in Greenville, removing Aubrey's uniform. His bedside clock told him it was just after two o'clock in the morning.

"Jack? It's Laura. Sorry for the late call. I need some of your professional help."

Wide awake now, Jack sat up in bed. "Of course. What's up?"

Laura was silent for a moment. "There's no easy way to say this. You remember my telling you that my dad asked me to help him if his condition got very bad?"

"Sure. And you told me that things were getting worse."

"Yes. Well, tonight I made a decision." There was silence again. "Tonight I helped him."

It took Jack a moment to realize what Laura meant. "You mean you—"

"That's right. I just finished. He's gone."

"You're sure? Well, that's a stupid thing for me to say to a doctor. Don't do anything. I'll be right over. Oh, is it okay if I bring Homes with me?"

"Of course. I think I'm going to need all the help I can get. Oh, I'm at dad's apartment. You remember where that is?"

"Yes. I'll be right there."

Laura was waiting for them when Jack and Homes arrived. Jack could tell she was trying hard to appear calm and relaxed.

"This is a hell of a way for us to finally meet, Dr. Benjamin," Homes said, extending his hand.

Laura smiled briefly at him. "It's good to have you here, Homes. And please call me Laura."

Homes nodded. "Have you called anyone or moved anything?"

"No. Jack said not to do anything."

"That's good. I'm going to phone this in now. That will bring a shitload of officers down on us, and I suspect they'll have to take you to the department."

Laura nodded. "I thought as much."

"Laura, this might be a good time to call your attorney," Jack said.

Homes nodded his agreement and then began talking to someone at the main precinct.

"I've been talking a good deal to one lately. Barbara Desmond—you may know her," Laura said.

"I do know her," Jack said, remembering that they had dated for a few months several years ago. "Assisted suicide is her specialty, I think."

"That's right. She won't be surprised at my call." Laura walked a few steps away and picked up her cell phone.

"Homes, I'm trying to remember. Didn't the Georgia Supreme Court overrule and throw out the state's law banning assisted suicide a few years ago? Maybe Laura will be okay."

Homes shook his head. "Sorry, but two months after the court threw out the old law, the state legislature passed a new, tougher one, and the governor signed it. Now it's felony murder, second degree. That's twenty-five years minimum if she's convicted. This law is really hard-ass, Jack. No exceptions—and you know how conservative this state is."

Jack nodded. "I remember that new law now. I don't like the sound of it."

Laura walked back to the two men. "Barb said she'll be right over. Should I call a doctor or anything?"

"Not right now," Homes said. "Let my guys do their thing first. That will take some time. Then you'll be able to make the call and maybe take care of any arrangements, too."

The Roswell police arrived a few minutes later, greeted Homes and Jack, and got to work. One officer brought Laura into a spare bedroom to question her privately. Photographers and a coroner busied themselves with the body.

When there was another knock at the door, Jack guessed it might be Barb Desmond; he walked over and opened it. They hugged each other briefly—they had parted as good friends when they'd stopped dating—and Jack introduced her to Homes.

"Where's Laura now?" Barb asked.

"She's in a spare bedroom, being questioned by Detective Stabler," Homes said.

Barb's brow wrinkled. "They should have waited for me." She headed for the bedroom, knocked once, opened the door, and went in.

"Now it's hurry up and wait, isn't it, Homes?"

"Yeah, you remember the drill. The real question is whether or not they'll release Laura after they bring her in and book her."

Jack nodded. "It's a crime on the books no matter how we may feel about it personally."

Homes agreed. "And our asshole of a DA, Dan Glover, loves these kinds of cases. He's thinking about running for governor soon, and the publicity from this situation is made to order for him."

When Laura left the bedroom with Detective Stabler and Barb, they walked over to Homes and Jack. "Homes, you know we've got to take her in and book her. The scene is pretty clean here, and our people don't have any questions, so there's no mystery about what happened. I think Ms. Benjamin will be released unless something comes up I'm not aware of."

"Yeah, thanks, Stabler. We'll all head downtown right behind you," Homes said.

Stabler nodded and turned to Laura. "Ms. Benjamin, I'll apologize in advance for having to do this, but I've got to cuff you before we leave. Standard procedure in cases like this."

Laura nodded as she extended her wrists, and tears welled up in her eyes. Barb patted her arm. "I'll see you downtown in a minute, Laura," she said.

Laura and Stabler headed for the door of the apartment, followed by Barb.

Jack and Homes walked out to Jack's car and climbed in. "This is a bunch of shit to go through for anyone, and I hate it for Laura. She's a genuinely nice person," Jack said.

Homes nodded.

"What kind of a guy is Stabler? He was just joining the force when I was leaving," Jack said.

"He's a good man. Takes a lot of kidding over having the same last name as that guy on television—that *Law and Order* guy."

"I bet he does."

"They're always asking him why he never nailed that chick he works with on the show—what's her name?"

"Olivia."

"Yeah, that's it. He's getting pretty tired of it."

They drove the rest of the way in silence.

J ack and Laura were seated in Barb Desmond's law office, discussing
the case. Laura had been formally charged with second-degree
murder and released on her own recognizance after posting
$100,000 bail. She had made her calls to the family doctor and to a
funeral home for arrangements for her father.

"The bail might have been higher, or Judge Benson could have
ruled there would be no bail at all," Barb said. "We were fortunate to
draw Benson. She knows the law and is fair and impartial. The feelings
about assisted suicide are a bit mixed among our judges, if not among
the general population of Georgia."

Jack cleared his throat. "DA Glover certainly lived up to being an
asshole, handling the case in person and asking the judge to refuse bail."

Barb nodded. "Yes, we figured something like that would happen."

"Barb, what's the worst-case scenario in this situation?" Laura's
concern showed in her voice.

"As the judge explained, assisted suicide is a felony in Georgia. It's
second-degree murder. The penalty is a minimum of twenty-five years
if you're convicted."

Laura put her face in her hands. "Is that it?"

"No. As a health-care provider, it's also possible to have your license
to practice revoked. That could come as a recommendation from the jury
or the judge. You can bet the DA will be pushing for that on the remote
chance you're convicted."

Jack had been holding Laura's hand throughout the conversation,
and he could feel her grip tightening as Barb spoke.

"Laura, I don't think that's going to happen, and I've handled a lot of these cases. The person involved wasn't a former lover or someone with whom you'd had a violent disagreement. You loved your father, and he loved you. We have his letters to you asking—begging, really—that you help him pass. You told me he was in pain the last few weeks from his cancer, and the formal autopsy will explain all of that. He had no estate of any consequence, so there's no motive there. He's had a living will for years and appointed you as his health-care proxy. Georgia juries have been about fifty-fifty on accepting those documents favorably, so we have at least a decent chance there. As a psychiatrist, you are also an MD, so there's no question about your medical competency. These are all good things."

"Still, according to Georgia law, I'm a murderer. Even if I'm acquitted, how can I hope to practice around here in the future?"

"Don't be too quick to assume that," Barb said. "My experience has been that decent people will come to you for help of all kinds because your patience and sensitivity and compassion will have been proven. This thing can work both ways. I know there doesn't seem to be a light at the end of the tunnel right now, but there is. Something else may work in our favor. The judge is allowing cameras in the courtroom. Your attractive appearance and sympathetic manner are a big positive for us."

"Barb's right, Laura," Jack said. "This is by no means a done deal. You have a lot of supportive people who will testify and back you up."

"What happens next, Barb?"

"Well, you've been arraigned, and the judge has set a trial date for three months from now. We shouldn't need more time. Just go about your business as usual, but taking some time off for a while isn't a bad idea either. Don't speak to reporters, especially television reporters. Don't be seen out in public drinking or laughing hysterically. That may sound stupid, but it has happened."

"No problem there," Laura said. "What else?"

"We'll be in the district court in downtown Atlanta. The grand jury will issue an indictment, which is standard procedure in these types of felony cases. Next is all lawyer stuff. The DA goes through discovery and is supposed to give me all the information his office has collected in its investigation. They seldom do, but that's the law. This process has just begun. We'll share our information as well, many of the items and issues I've just outlined."

"Is that the reason the judge set ninety days for the trial?"

"Yes, that's one of them. It's also a good sign that the judge doesn't see any severe complications in this case, because there are none. The DA will try to make it sound like there are some, of course. He may ask for a plea bargain at that point, which we will reject. You're not guilty, Laura, and we won't play games with the DA on that score."

Laura smiled for the first time. "Thanks for that, Barb."

Barb nodded. "I think you know me well enough, Laura, to believe that I don't BS my clients. If I thought you were in real trouble, I'd tell you so. After all that, we'll be ready for trial."

"Barb, can I ask a personal question?" Jack said.

"Of course."

"I think you know that Laura and I have been dating and that I was previously a patient of hers."

"Yes, Laura has told me all that."

"How public should we be about our relationship? I want to go on seeing Laura when she feels ready for that, but I don't want to compromise her in any way."

"I think your continued relationship is fine. You might wait a couple of weeks before doing things publicly." Barb cleared her throat. "Laura also told me that you've stopped drinking, and that's a good thing."

Jack smiled at her. "I'd agree with that. So it's not an issue."

"Good. Any other questions, Laura?"

Laura stood up, shaking her head. "I don't think so. I'll call you if I think of anything."

"Yes, you know you can call me for any reason. You already have my cell-phone number, and I'll answer it at any time."

Jack and Laura shook hands with Barb and left her office.

Jack waited for a moment before he started his car. "Laura, I know it's early, but what do you say we have an early dinner and call it a night?"

She reached across and patted Jack's knee. "That's sweet of you. I think a good night's sleep is just what I need. This may sound silly, but why don't we get some Chick-fil-A sandwiches and go back to my place? That's about all I feel like right now."

Jack pulled out into traffic. "You sure? That's okay with me, but I'm willing to spend some big bucks on you at, oh, Wendy's." He saw her smile.

"No, a chicken sandwich sounds just right."

Back in her apartment, Laura put their sandwiches on plates, added some coleslaw she had made the day before, and poured herself a glass of white wine. "What will you have to drink, Jack?"

"Water will be fine for me," he said, starting to get up from the living-room sofa.

"That's okay," she said. "I'll bring this to you. Excuse me for a minute." Laura went into the bathroom with her purse and then returned and brought their meals over to Jack. She sat beside him, had a sip of wine, and sighed. "I know Barb was being positive, but it was pretty brutal listening to all the things that could go wrong."

"Remember what she kept saying; you have a lot of positives on your side and no negatives. Great slaw, by the way."

"Thanks. I know that's what she said, but I wonder about what the DA may find or even make up."

"He does have a reputation for that. You don't strike me as having had a deep, dark past." Jack smiled, and they talked about other things. Finally, he finished his sandwich.

"Want anything else?" Laura asked.

"No, I'm good."

Laura took their plates into the kitchen, hesitated for a moment, and then poured herself a half glass of wine. One was usually her limit. "I really don't have a past," she said. She walked back to the sofa and sat beside Jack. "I'm certainly no angel, but I've been a pretty good girl." Jack watched her blush and reached over for her hand.

"Ready to change that a little?"

While they had been dating for a few weeks, their relationship hadn't turned sexual yet, but both of them knew it was coming.

Laura sipped more of her wine and put her arms around Jack's neck. "I think I'm more than ready."

He leaned into her and tasted the wine on her lips, surprised at the mild jolt he felt at the strength of her kiss as well as the urgency of her body. The alcohol didn't taste bad either as their tongues met.

Laura guided his hands where she wanted them, and she wanted them everywhere. As things grew more intense, she drew slowly away, stood up, and took his hand. "Jack, it's been a long time for me. I may not—"

"You'll be fine," he said.

She led him into her bedroom and lit two tall candles by her bed.

"I hope you don't mind. Part of the feminine mystique." She pulled him toward her, kissed him, and started to unbutton his shirt. Jack reached up to help her. "No. Let me," she said.

When she had removed his clothes and he had slipped out of his shoes, she moved a step back from him and slowly started to remove her own clothes. She went through the motions deliberately, watching him carefully, and then moved toward him.

Despite the low lighting in the bedroom, Jack marveled at how lovely she was. He started to kneel down in front of her, but she pulled him up and began to massage him slowly as they embraced intensely. Finally, she walked toward the bed and held her arms out to him. He joined her and was startled again at the level of her passion. He had only known her as the tranquil and composed psychiatrist who always appeared unruffled. Now her small cries turned to shouts as they rocked back and forth until they climaxed together. Turning to each other, they kissed softly. "Jack, you're so tender. That was lovely."

"For me too," he said, feeling only a little guilty about his recent visits to Aubrey.

The decision to have Laura testify was mutually agreed upon. During the three months before the trial began, Barb and Laura went over every facet of Laura's life since her childhood. Barb quizzed her about her earliest memories and then her love life, including an engagement that had lasted almost two years. Her academic record was flawless, and her psychiatric practice had received the highest marks in the annual reviews from her professional associations. Barb asked all the tough questions she knew the DA would ask, even the impertinent ones, bringing Laura to tears several times. At the end of it, Barb was convinced that Laura's openness and honesty would win the jury over and assure her acquittal.

Judge Gloria Benson was a tall, striking black woman in her early forties. She had been in private practice in Atlanta for twelve years as a successful defense attorney. She was known for being tough and ran her trials smoothly and quickly. The trial was reaching the end of the first week, with Jack in attendance whenever his workload permitted. Barb was ready to call on Laura and, if things went as she hoped, rest her case for the defense. District Attorney Glover, while being his usual surly self, was surprisingly low-key. His witnesses were as expected, and it was obvious he was leaning on the strong Georgia law prohibiting assisted suicide for all the support he needed. He had called the two state legislators who had authored the law to explain their motivation, as well as several well-known legal authorities who proclaimed the law to be constitutionally sound and valid. He had made a good case, but Barb felt it was morally bankrupt. There had been no discussion of the human beings involved—Laura and her father—and what must be the deeper moral issue: one loving human being helping another. At that point, Barb called Laura to the stand.

Barb went through the usual preliminaries, establishing Laura's bona fides and letting her discuss her devoted relationship with her father and the time she had spent caring for him. Barb also offered into evidence the father's letters to Laura asking for her help in ending his life when the time came. Her testimony took almost three hours, at which point the judge announced a two-hour adjournment for lunch.

When the court returned, it was District Attorney Glover's turn, and he seemed revitalized and as if he relished the opportunity to question Laura. Barb had warned her that the questioning would be more of an interrogation.

"Ms. Benjamin, will you please restate some of your background for the jury? It's been a long day, and they may have forgotten."

"Certainly," Laura said. "And I prefer Dr. Benjamin, please."

"Of course," the DA said, smiling. "Dr. Benjamin, you're not a Georgia native, are you?"

"No. I'm originally from Massachusetts."

"Yes, now I recall," he said, flipping through blank pages in his notes to appear as if he had something important written there. "And the town you lived in?"

"I lived in Marlborough most of my early life."

"What part of the state is that in, Doctor?"

Barb wondered what Glover was up to and studied him carefully. He never asked irrelevant questions unless he was after something.

"Marlborough is in northeast Massachusetts."

"And you lived there until you were how old?"

Laura was calm and focused. Barb had warned her that Glover would probably lay some traps, and she had not let down her guard.

"Until I was five or six—I really can't remember."

"I see. Your Honor, I would like to introduce into evidence two new pieces of information just received by my office."

"Objection, Your Honor." Barb was on her feet and mad as hell. This was a typical Glover tactic. He had not shared any of this evidence with her, and she knew he had concealed it intentionally.

"Both attorneys, please approach," the judge announced.

When Barb and DA Glover stood before her, the judge switched off her microphone and looked sternly at Glover. She glanced briefly at the two documents. "You know better than this, Dan. And I've seen you try this before. You should have given a copy of this information to Ms. Desmond weeks or even months ago."

"Your Honor, as I said, my office has just received this information, although we requested it quite some time ago. I apologize to the court."

Barb was livid. "Your Honor, please don't allow Mr. Glover to pull one of his too-familiar tricks when my client's reputation and freedom are at stake."

The judge thought for a moment. "Mr. Glover, I want to go over this material in detail in my chambers with both of you present. I'm going to adjourn court for the day, and I'll see the two of you immediately."

In chambers, the judge removed her judicial robe. "Honest to God, Dan, how many times do you think you can get away with this last-minute shit? Give me this so-called new information." She sat behind her desk.

Glover handed over a small newspaper clipping and a longer legal-looking document. The judge read the clipping quickly, turned to the legal document and read it carefully, and, finally, handed it to Barb.

After a moment, Barb was quick to respond. "Your Honor, I'm going to need some time to verify this information. At least five days."

"I object to that length of time, Your Honor," Glover said, smiling.

"Barb, you've got two days, starting tomorrow. We'll reconvene on Friday."

17.

arb and Laura sat in Barb's office, the two documents on the desk. "Why didn't you tell me about this?" Barb asked Laura.

"I don't know anything about that clipping or about any domestic abuse. I must have been four or five at the time. I never heard anything about it."

"Your mother never brought it up?"

"No. Never. And I never remember my mother and father being separated or even having an argument."

"I have two of my paralegals checking this information out. It could mean nothing. At worst, it could suggest a motive for your later actions."

Laura shook her head. "Motive? There was nothing. Nothing!"

"But the DA will make something out of it—you can count on that. The fact that there was some kind of incident and your father was charged with domestic abuse is significant. That suggests a motive for the assisted suicide—that you hated your father for years because of the so-called abuse. But I can probably deal with that. This second thing is more serious. You should have told me about the abortion."

"The abortion was done privately when I was engaged and in grad school. I didn't think there was any record."

"There's *always* a record, Laura. For God's sake. You're a smart woman. Why would you think this wasn't important?"

"I don't see—"

"Well, let me lay it out for you again. The DA will use the news clipping to suggest you had a grudge against your father."

"That's ridiculous."

"Maybe it is to you, but it may not be to the jury. Glover will make it sound like you've been festering over this all your life. But the abortion—that's even worse."

"How so?" Laura was nervous.

"Come, come, Doctor. Can't you see Glover using your abortion as proof you have little regard for human life?"

"What!"

"I'm serious, Laura. Glover is good at this kind of thing."

"But it was all done legally!"

Barb shook her head. "That's not the point. The point will be that you took a life before—a life you had control over—so taking your father's life later on, which you also controlled, was no big deal."

"That's a lie!" Laura shouted.

"When Glover starts in on you, it may begin to sound very logical to the jury, most of whom are at least mildly conservative. I'm telling you the truth. This is bad shit, and right now, I don't know what to do about it."

18.

T he man now called Stone arrived in Birmingham without incident. He rented a car at the airport, made a few inquiries about motels nearby, and drove to one of the closest, a cheap nonchain property. As was his usual ritual, he stripped the bed and replaced its shabby coverings with his own red silk sheets. He quickly reviewed the information about Carson Weber and then listened again to the Arie Clavin tape to put himself in the mood for his next adventure.

Stone reached Weber's home in the early afternoon. His investigative files had warned him that Weber seldom came to his door, so Stone persistently rang the doorbell and knocked loudly until Weber finally answered. Weber's face was filled with pain; he was a defeated man. Stone informed Weber that he was an insurance representative from Memphis and was going to present him with a sizable insurance payment resulting from the death of his granddaughter, Sharon. Stone said the policy had only recently been discovered and he did not know who had taken out the policy and made Mr. Weber the beneficiary, but if Weber would allow him inside his home, Stone would look through his paperwork to see if he could locate the information. Again, Stone flashed a sincere smile.

Weber became extremely upset at the thought that he might receive any benefit from Sharon's death, when he felt he had caused her death. As he began to weep, he said he would not accept any payment. Stone assured him that one suitable disposition of the proceeds might be to create a memorial fund or charitable contribution in Sharon's name. This was little comfort, and Weber cried openly as Stone sifted through fictitious paperwork in his briefcase while checking to see that his tape recorder was functioning. Smiling and appearing sympathetic, Stone suggested that a drink of water might help to settle Mr. Weber and that he would appreciate some water himself. When Weber returned with the water, Stone asked him if he had a picture of Sharon for his records. Weber, who had begun crying again, excused himself to locate a photograph. In a quick, practiced motion, Stone added a small vial of Neuromaxim to Weber's water.

When Weber was seated again, Stone prompted the man to tell him about Sharon and how the accident had occurred. Weber continued sniveling and choking as he relived the tragedy, taking frequent large sips of water. In a short time, he slumped to the side of his sofa, unable to move, puzzled eyes wide open. Stone tested the drug's effectiveness by slapping Weber sharply across the face. The man never moved or made a sound. Tears streamed from his eyes.

Stone was tired of Weber's crying, silently or not. Inflicting pain without responsive sound was a waste of time. Stone mentally reviewed the various methods he could use to bring about the results he wanted and needed to hear: the sounds of agony and hysteria. Weber's persistent sniveling had already been recorded, and time was limited before the drug wore off. He could use some drugs he always brought with him for emergencies, but he had hoped to end Weber's life in the swimming pool where his granddaughter had died. It was always his preference to duplicate the irony of the previous death. But time was the key factor, and it was running out. Sighing sadly, Stone admitted to himself that it would be best to concede that this attempt had been a failure and that he should conclude the event quickly and return to Kill Devil Hills to prepare for his next—hopefully more satisfactory—event.

Mr. Weber's swimming pool was visible from the living room behind a screened enclosure. Stone walked over to the entrance door, blocked it open with a chair, and then returned to Weber on the sofa. He planned to pull Weber's body over to the pool, push him in, and leave. Unable to control himself in any way, Weber would slowly drown, eyes wide open. There was some pleasurable irony, Stone thought, in Weber's dying in the same way Sharon had—and in the same location, not unlike Arie Clavin and her father. Stone enjoyed ironies. They were good omens.

He grabbed both of Weber's legs and slowly pulled them onto the floor. Weber's head unexpectedly slipped from the sofa and landed jarringly on the floor, facedown. *Damn!* Stone did not normally use profane language but he was tempted to do so as he saw blood begin to flow from Weber's mouth and nose. Using his handkerchief, Stone stopped the flow as best he could, righted Weber's head, and pulled him toward the door to the pool. Once inside the screened enclosure, he wiped Weber's face once more and pushed him into the water. He watched the body float facedown. There was no movement or sound. *Such a shame.* More than that, Stone needed the emotional relief he usually experienced from his visits. This one was a total loss.

Walking back into the living room, Stone decided to clean the area where Weber had bled onto the floor. He found a dish towel in the kitchen, moistened it, came back into the living room, and carefully wiped clean any trace of blood from the sofa to the door to the pool. He opened his briefcase, turned off the recorder, and placed the wet dish towel inside. He removed the glasses of water, rinsed them in the kitchen sink, carefully wiped them clean, and replaced them on a shelf. Glancing quickly around the living room, he looked through a window up and down the quiet street, and then he left the Weber home, got into his rental car, and headed directly for the Birmingham airport. With any luck, he could catch an earlier flight to Norfolk and then back home. He regretted not having anything interesting to listen to on his recorder as a reward for his time spent with Mr. Weber. He was already feeling a growing compulsion to find another victim—quickly.

19

J udge Benson seated herself and looked around the court. She had
been told that several jurors were upset at the delay in the trial, but
that didn't concern her. To her, jury duty was an essential part of
citizenship. What did bother her was the direction the trial might take
when the new information was presented to the jury. Judge Benson did
not agree with the Georgia law concerning assisted suicide, but it was
the law. Now she felt the DA would attempt to direct the jury's mind to
abortion rather than to the assisted-suicide charge. She would preside over
this trial fairly, charge the jury carefully, and trust the jury's verdict. But
she would keep a closer eye on DA Glover, a man she had never liked.

"Mr. Glover, are you ready to continue your cross-examination?"

"I am, Your Honor."

"Please proceed."

Glover turned to Laura in the witness stand. "Good morning, Ms.
Benjamin—I mean Dr. Benjamin." His smile was more of a smirk.

"Good morning."

"We've been gone a few days, so I want to refresh the jurors' minds
about where we left off. I believe you had just told us that you lived your
early years in the town of Marlborough, Massachusetts. Is that correct?"

"Yes." Barb had admonished Laura to keep her replies simple and
to use one-word responses when she could.

Glover nodded. "I have here a clipping from the Marlborough
newspaper dated April 8, 1985. This is state's exhibit three, Your Honor."
He handed a copy to the judge and to Barb. He took the clipping to the
witness box and handed it to Laura. "Dr. Benjamin, will you please read
the clipping aloud to the jury?"

Laura had read the clipping many times over the past two days, and Barb had coached her on her possible replies and warned her to be wary of Glover. She was hesitant but cleared her throat and began. "'Police were called to the home of Daniel Benjamin, 36 Cowell Drive, yesterday, responding to a complaint about a family dispute. Benjamin, thirty-eight, was arrested and charged with domestic abuse. His wife, Emily, was the complaining party.'" Laura's face was bright red as she stopped reading.

"Dr. Benjamin, is the Daniel Benjamin in the article your father?"

Laura was silent for a moment, gathering her composure. "I-I've never seen this before."

"That wasn't the question, Doctor. Was the Daniel Benjamin in the article your father—yes or no?"

"That was our address, but I've never heard of this."

"That is your father's name, is it not?"

"Yes."

"And you said you had never heard of this incident?"

"That's right. I was five."

"You have no memories of you or your mother being beaten or abused by your father?"

"Objection!" Barb had been ready for this kind of insinuation by Glover and was on her feet, her face as red as Laura's. "The article did not mention any beatings or that the child was involved."

"Sustained. Be careful, Mr. Glover."

Glover nodded at the judge. "So you have no memory of that incident?"

"No. I was only five."

"And your mother never discussed it with you?"

"No."

"Not over the many years after you had grown up? You had no resentment toward your father for this"—he paused to glance at the clipping—"abuse?"

"Objection. Asked and answered."

"Sustained. Move on, Mr. Glover."

"Now, Dr. Benjamin, can you tell the jury where you went to college?"

"College? Well, I went to several colleges—undergrad and then for my master's and doctorate."

"You were engaged during that period? Engaged to be married?"

"Yes."

Glover walked back to his desk and withdrew a white sheet of paper from a file. "Your Honor, I'm going to introduce into evidence a medical report for Laura Benjamin, who was twenty-five years old at the time of this incident and attending Boston University. This will be state's exhibit four." He delivered copies as he had previously, handing one again to Laura.

"Dr. Benjamin, you are a medical doctor?"

"Yes, I am." Laura knew what was coming.

"Will you please tell the jury what this document is?"

"It's a medical report—a statement of a medical procedure."

"And what was that procedure?"

"It was for a termination of pregnancy." There was a noticeable murmur in the courtroom.

"You mean an abortion, don't you?" Glover turned to the jury with his best disapproving expression.

"That's another term for the same thing."

Glover was annoyed. "And who was this abortion—this termination of life—performed upon?"

"Objection! Your Honor, the medical community differs on whether or not this procedure terminates a life or not in the early stages." Barb was furious.

"Sustained. The jury will disregard the phrase 'termination of life.'"

Now Glover was mad. "Your Honor, I will call numerous doctors and clergymen who will testify that abortion at any time *is* a termination of life."

"Mr. Glover, you may present your witnesses at the appropriate time. I have ruled on the objection. Please proceed."

"Fine. Will the witness please tell the jury whose name is on the medical report as having received the abortion?"

Laura took her time replying, trying to control her emotions. "Laura Benjamin."

"That is your name, is it not, Doctor?"

Laura nodded. "Yes."

"So you had an abortion when you were twenty-five. You ended the—your pregnancy. Is that correct?"

"Yes."

"You did away with the child within your body."

"Objection!" Barb said.

The judge rapped her gavel several times. "The court will come to order. Mr. Glover, I have already stated that you can present your medical witnesses at the proper time concerning whether or not the fetus was a child. The jury will disregard the phrase at this time."

Glover paced back and forth before the witness stand. "Dr. Benjamin, as a medical doctor, would you give us your opinion as to the relationship between a termination of pregnancy and assisted suicide?"

"Objection, Your Honor. Objection!" Barb was livid. Laura had begun to cry.

"Mr. Glover, you are out of order and in contempt. We'll discuss your penalty after adjournment today," said the judge.

Glover seemed unconcerned. He only paused briefly before attacking Laura again.

"Dr. Benjamin, will you please tell the court what religion you profess?"

"Objection, Your Honor! Irrelevant and immaterial," Barb said.

Glover responded quickly. "Your Honor, what this witness believes and practices as a matter of personal conviction is extremely relevant and pertains directly to this witness's moral character and what issues are at the very heart of this case—matters of life and death."

The judge considered this for a moment. "Objection overruled. Dr. Benjamin, you may answer the question."

Laura had begun to cry again. "I'm a Catholic."

Glover, of course, had known what her reply would be. "A Catholic? I see. And doesn't the Catholic faith prohibit abortion—prohibit the termination of pregnancy—under all circumstances?"

Laura tried to stop crying.

"Dr. Benjamin, did you hear the question?" Glover was going for the kill.

"Yes. The church does oppose abortion."

Again, the rumble of conversation in the courtroom could clearly be heard. One of the jurors had lowered her head and was weeping.

"So in terminating your pregnancy, in aborting your fetus, you went directly against the dictates of a religion you profess to believe in, as you also did in taking your father's life."

Laura had had enough. She stood up in the witness stand. Raising her voice, almost shouting, she said, "Yes! Yes, I did. I loved my father. I tried to help him. He begged me to help him. And under the circumstances, I would do it again."

Barb was also on her feet. "Object to the line of questioning, Your Honor. My client is not on trial for abortion."

The courtroom was close to being out of control, and the judge rapped her gavel several times until she received full quiet. "We'll continue testimony tomorrow. I'd like to see counsel in my chambers. The court is adjourned."

20.

Homes walked into Jack's office without knocking and found his friend working at his computer.

"Hey, what's up?" Jack said.

"Didn't mean to interrupt your search for pornography," Homes said. "Got something for you."

"Yeah, what?"

Homes flipped a file onto Jack's desk and sat down. "Jesus, you'd think you'd get some comfortable chairs in this office."

"Sure, like those torture devices in your office at the station." Jack glanced at the file and then started reading. "What's this all about?"

"Thought it was interesting. Came over the regional wire this morning."

Jack nodded as he continued reading. "So this old guy in Birmingham drowned himself in his pool, distraught because he had let his grandkid drown in the same pool. So what?"

Homes sighed. "Just a feeling. Doesn't something about it sound familiar—like Pendleton? It just don't make sense. It's been almost three years since the kid died. So why did the guy wait that long? These kinds of suicides—they usually happen right after the first death. A guy's wife dies, and he kills himself within a few days or weeks afterward. A kid dies, and one or both of the parents pulls the plug. Not many wait three years."

Jack nodded. "Maybe. Kind of weak, though. Arie Clavin waited, what, thirty years?"

"Your ass is weak," Homes said. "And we don't know that Arie Clavin waited and wasn't murdered. How about this? The report says the guy was fully clothed and had his watch on, his pockets weren't empty, and no alcohol or drugs were in his system."

"So?"

"Jack, don't you remember any of your cop training? People don't usually drown themselves fully dressed with all their ID in their pockets. Not if they're conscious. And they usually take something—booze or drugs—to help them do the deed. On the other hand, a murderer doesn't care about emptying pockets."

"Some suicides don't care either," Jack said.

"Yeah, some don't, but not many. He didn't leave a note either. If he was so damned depressed three years after the fact, why no note?"

"Homes, for Christ's sake, none of this means anything."

"Here's the clincher for me, Jackie: the coroner's report says he had a blow to his face. He had been bleeding."

"So he had a blackout and then slipped and fell into the pool."

Homes shook his head. "I don't think so. Report says he was in generally good physical health. I think it's worth checking out."

"So go check it out, and let me get back to my pornography." Jack turned to his computer.

"Why don't I take the day off, and we'll both drive over to Birmingham to see what we can find?"

"Homes, there's nothing to find. I've got work to do."

Homes stood up. "Work, my ass. I've got this buddy in the coroner's office down there—Andy Page. Used to work with me here in Roswell. I called him awhile ago, and he said to come down, and he'll show us the whole thing—the house, the pool, the body. What's the drive down there—two, three hours?"

"About, yeah. But what for?"

"Jack, something about this don't make sense to me. Like that thing in Pendleton. That Clavin dame kills herself the same way her father killed himself—and in the same place. Now this guy in Birmingham drowns himself in the same pool where his little granddaughter died. It bothers me. So humor me. We can have some barbecue at that great place down there. What is it?"

"Dreamland, but we've got one of their restaurants right here in Roswell."

"It ain't as good, though. The Birmingham one is the original."

Jack started laughing. "And you're an original too—an original jerk off." Jack made a few clicks with his mouse and shut down the computer. "Okay, I don't have to be at Laura's trial until tomorrow, so let's drive to Birmingham."

At the central police station in Birmingham, the coroner, Andy Page, and Homes exchanged BS for a few minutes, and then Page asked what they wanted to see first.

"How about the body?" Jack said.

"Good enough," Page said. "Follow me."

The three men went down two flights of stairs into what looked like a hospital operating room. Page walked over to a large row of stainless-steel cabinets, opened one, and slid out a sheet-covered body. He pulled back the covering, and Homes and Jack moved up for a closer look.

"Poor old bastard," Page said, shaking his head.

"Yeah," Homes replied. "Any new info since the report you faxed me, Andy?"

"Not really. There was a big fight in the family when the kid died under his watch. Now his next of kin won't even claim the old man's body. He had a few bucks, and he'll be buried properly, but it's a real shame. I'm still puzzled a little about the abrasions to his nose and mouth. He also has one on the side of his face—like he might have been slapped."

"How the hell can you tell that, Andy?"

"We can tell a lot of shit now that we couldn't just a few years ago, Homes. Capillaries break under the skin with any bruise. The marks on his cheek indicate a pretty good whack. If it was a slap, he sure as hell didn't slap himself."

"Any needle marks on him, Andy?" Jack had moved up closer to the body.

"Nope. And we checked for any minute marks in between his fingers and toes, in his hair under his arms, and in his pubes. He was clean. Blood was clean too. Complete autopsy showed he was in damn good health for a guy his age—late sixties. No heart problems. Nothing."

"In other words, we don't have shit," Homes said.

"That's about it. None of our guys thought it was anything but suicide. Our techs found some interesting stuff in the house, though. It's only a few minutes from here. Let's drive over, and I'll show you."

Page walked them around the house, pointing out anything of interest.

"Looks pretty clean here, too," Homes said.

"Maybe," Andy replied. "Take a look at this."

He turned off the living-room light. "Homes, hold the UV light for me, will you?"

"Sure. Luminol time, huh?"

"A little magic goes a long way, buddy." He sprayed an area on the living-room floor in between the table and the sofa. "Okay, hit the light."

The UV light showed several smears of blood on the floor. "So we know there was blood on the floor, and somebody tried to wipe it up. You can never get rid of all of it, Homes, as you know."

"Yeah, so somebody could have bumped the old guy off."

"Or he cut himself, or he got a bloody nose, and it leaked onto the floor while he sat on the sofa and tried to clean it up himself," Jack said.

"No cuts anywhere on the body. The blood is fresh, so it isn't from some old wound. We know it's his blood type, but we can't really tell anything else."

"It still stinks to me," Homes said.

"Here's something else. May be nothing," Andy said. "Two rings on the table from glasses. Homes, you know what a nosy bastard I was when we worked together in Roswell. Always trying to find shit at a crime scene."

"Yeah, I remember. You shoulda been a detective." They both laughed.

"Here's my point," Andy said. "This guy lived alone. Neighbors said he didn't have friends or visitors. Never. When the kid died, everybody cut him off—family and neighbors. His daughter and son-in-law told our detectives the same thing. So why two glass rings on the table?"

"Hell, they could be years old," Jack said.

"Nope. We can tell that difference. These are fairly new. Come in the kitchen," Page said.

They walked a few steps into the kitchen. It was remarkably neat and clean.

"Damn, I wish my place was this clean," Homes said.

"If you weren't such a messy bastard, it would be," Jack said, punching his friend on the arm.

"Homes, I know you love a mystery. Maybe this is one." Andy opened all of the kitchen cabinets and stepped back.

"Yeah, so?" Homes said, looking over the cabinets.

Page pointed to the glasses on one shelf. "Here's where he kept all his water glasses. So why are these two glasses out of place?" He gestured toward a couple of glasses stuck awkwardly in between some cereal bowls on another shelf.

"Maybe he was in a hurry," Homes said.

"To kill himself? I don't think so. He hadn't done it for three years. And nothing else in this house is out of order—not his suits in the closet, not his underwear in his drawers. Even his shoes are lined up neatly in his closet. Bathroom is immaculate. This guy had nothing else to do, so he kept things arranged neatly. Perfectly."

"Except for these glasses," Jack said.

"Yeah. And if I was the suspicious type, I'd say somebody else who didn't know the layout put them glasses away—somebody who was in a hurry. And here's the thing that really bugs me."

"Jesus, Andy, you're more hung up on this thing than I am," Homes said.

"Just think about this. When you guys empty your dishwasher, how do you put the dishes away?"

"That's easy," Jack said. "Homes never puts any dishes away. He selects his dishes right out of the dishwasher—if he uses a dish."

Andy laughed. "No, but really, what do you do?"

"You pick things up and put them where they belong. But you already said—"

"Yeah, the neat stuff. But this is different. We didn't find any prints on the two glasses that're on the wrong shelf. Every other glass and dish has prints from Weber. That makes sense because we all take the dishes from the machine and put them on the shelf. So how come these two glasses have no prints?"

"He could have just wiped them off," Jack said.

"But why? He didn't wipe any others off. Why these two glasses? And here's another thing."

Andy took the two glasses out of the cabinet and walked back into the living room. "Here," he said, placing them on the small table. "They fit the rings. So how come Mr. Clean—Mr. Perfect—doesn't wipe the table off?"

"Jack says suicides don't always neaten up, Andy."

"These types do, Homes. I just feel it in my gut that this guy would have left a perfect home before he did himself in. But he didn't."

"So what do the glasses and these rings on the table say to you, Andy?"

"Well, if I was as suspicious as you always are, Homes, I'd say it suggests that the old guy was having a drink with somebody not too long before he died. Then the visitor—just for fun, let's call him the murderer—picked the glasses up, went into the kitchen, washed them out, dried them, so no prints, and put them on the wrong shelf."

"Might have been a neighbor. Or maybe somebody was here trying to sell him something."

"Not this guy. Notice the sign on the lawn? 'No Vendors.' Another one on the window by the front door. Neighbors say he never let anybody in. Seldom answered the door. They told me the kids even stayed away from the house on Halloween."

"Jesus, Andy, you really are worse than I am. Even little things make you suspicious."

"Maybe I picked it up from you. One last thing. Hit the lights again."

Andy walked over to the screen door on the pool and flipped his UV light on. Homes and Jack joined him. Slowly, they walked back to the sofa.

"See those blood smears and other marks on the floor? The blood was Weber's, and the marks could be scuff marks. From shoes. Like he might have been dragged."

"Or he was dragging something out to the pool, and it was heavy. Maybe one of those tables or chairs," Jack said, "and Weber's nose was still bleeding."

"I don't think so," Andy said. "But I can't prove differently, and neither can our detectives. That's why this case is going to go down as a suicide."

Homes had a serious look on his face. "Andy, doesn't the fact that the blood was wiped up fit into the neatness thing? Wasn't the guy just trying to clean up before he took a dip in the pool?"

"Glad you mentioned that, Homes. If he did clean it up himself, then where's the bloody towel or rag? He's got two of every dish towel, and all of his other linens in this house. We only found one dish towel without a mate. And no bloody rags. Not even paper towels. We checked everywhere, including the inside and outside garbage cans. Nothing. I tell you it just doesn't fit."

The men left the house silently, all of them thinking over what they'd seen, trying to determine if it made any sense.

"Andy, how about going to Dreamland with us for some barbecue?" Homes asked his friend. "Maybe we can kick this around some more. Jack here is still skeptical."

"Sounds good to me. No beer for sale there, but the food will be great."

The three men talked over lunch, with Andy reiterating the points he had made in the house. Homes intermittently agreed with him. Jack had a few questions but was otherwise silent. Finally, he said what was on his mind.

"Guys, it seems to me that we're trying to make something fit that just doesn't fit. There are at least two explanations for everything Andy has found. We want them all to mean something and to lead us somewhere. But I just can't go with it. And I think part of the problem— and this is for Andy's information—is that Homes and I have had our heads in another case—actually, another suicide that gives us the same feel as this one. It keeps pulling at us, but we have nothing to go on. And that other case had a lot fewer clues than you have in this case. And as we've both said, neither of them is really a case."

Andy nodded. "Homes said something to me about your other deal when we talked before you drove down here. I don't have to tell you that this happens all the time in our business. We get a case—like you say, it may not even be a case—and something about it bothers us, and it stays in our minds forever. Certainly for months and years."

The two other men agreed. "Andy, Jack and I need to get back. How about if you stay in touch? If anything else develops, give me a call. And it's drinks and dinner on us when you get up to Roswell."

They left Dreamland, walked to their cars, shook hands, and headed for home.

Jack and Homes were only five minutes out of town, when Homes asked him to pull over.

"Jack, if we don't finish up on this case—"

"Homes, it's *not* a case."

"Okay. If we don't finish checking up on this situation, it's going to bug both of us."

"What's left to do?"

"What did you do in Pendleton? I mean the stuff before your all-nighter with the so-called law-enforcement people."

Jack had to laugh. "I checked a few rental-car places and a motel, but Pendleton is a lot smaller than Birmingham."

"I know that. You said he stayed close to the airport in Pendleton. So let's say we only check three of each, closest to the airport, in case the murderer flew in. You say he picked a cheap motel?"

"Yes, but that's all they have in Pendleton."

"Well, it's all we have to go on. We're about a mile from the airport now. Let's head over there and start checking. So pick three motels and three car rentals. If nothing develops, we head for Roswell."

"You're right about one thing, Homes," Jack said, starting the car. "If we don't at least try, it will bug us forever." He pulled out into the traffic.

They got lucky at the second motel, a cheap, shabby nonchain motel. Jack and Homes showed their IDs to the grizzled man at the desk.

"We're looking for a guy that may be involved in a homicide," Jack told the man. "I don't have much information, but here's what I know. In the past several days, have you had a man in his midthirties check in, spend the night, mess up his room, maybe tear the sheets from his bed? May have had a strange smile."

"Oh, that dude. Sure, just a few days ago. The thing with the sheets—that was weird." He started tapping on his computer keyboard. "Name is Gregory Stone. Insurance guy out of Memphis."

Jack crossed his fingers. "Any home or company address?"

"Company. Crossman and Blore, 1211 Holyrood, Memphis. That's it. Oh yeah, come to think of it, he did smile funny."

"Thanks. Where's your closest car rental?"

"Less than a half mile to the right out of here. Dollar, I think."

Jack and Homes practically ran out of the motel to their car.

"Jack, this fucker's got to be the same guy as in Pendleton. Got to."

"That's what I'm beginning to believe."

They went inside the Dollar car rental and up to the counter. An overweight redhead was sitting on a stool, smoking under a Thanks for Not Smoking sign. The two men went through their IDs and a brief explanation of what they were looking for.

"Over the past few days, did a Gregory Stone from Memphis rent a car from you?"

"Lemme see," the woman said, putting out her cigarette and turning to her computer. "I'll check the last thirty days. Sure. Here he is. Gregory Stone."

"Can you give me his driver's license number—better yet, a printout of his license and photo?" Jack crossed his fingers again.

"Sure. We like to cooperate with the cops—I mean with police officers." She made a quick copy and handed it to them.

Jack and Homes looked at the copy. Gregory Stone was not an unpleasant-looking man. The faint smile on his face did look odd.

"Jesus Christ, Jack," Homes said. "This is our guy."

Jack stared at the man's face. "Maybe. Maybe it's just Gregory Stone from Memphis."

He looked up at the woman. "Can I ask you to e-mail a copy of this license to police headquarters in Roswell, Georgia?"

"Sure. Only take a second." Homes handed a card with his e-mail to the woman.

"One more thing"—Jack looked at her name tag—"Betty. Do you know what airline he came in on?"

The woman tapped a few more keys. "It says Southwest here. Southwest flight 217."

"Thanks, Betty. If I had enough time, I'd ask you to marry me."

They thanked the woman again and walked out of the car rental.

"Jack, I'll bet you my entire retirement pension that this is the fucker we want. He's got to be. When we get back to the office, I'll run the license and then send his photo to the TBI in Tennessee and to the FBI. We're bound to get a hit."

"I hope you're right, Homes. This is the first break we've had. Look, it's four in the afternoon now and almost a three-hour ride back to Roswell, so let's hit the road. Maybe we can get some legit ID on this guy tonight."

"You took the words right out of my mouth, Jackie. We can get something to eat on the road."

Homes and Jack walked into the Roswell police station and went directly to Homes's office. The e-mail with the driver's license was waiting for him. He immediately ran the license through the nationwide database.

Nothing.

Then he ran the man's company in Memphis—Crossman and Blore.

Nothing.

"Holy shit, Jack. Mr. Nobody. We've got him."

"Got what, Homes? We don't really know who he is or where he lives. And the truth is, we don't know if this is the same guy as the one from Pendleton."

"Jack, tell me your gut isn't shouting at you about this guy," Homes said.

Jack smiled. "Yeah, it's yellin' at me loud and clear. But we have no proof, Homes, and no place to look for him."

Homes finished hitting some keys on his computer. "We will in the morning, Jackie boy. I just sent the license to the Tennessee Bureau of Investigation and to the FBI. I'm also checking out the origin of this Southwest flight 217. Bet you dinner we have this son of a bitch by noon tomorrow."

"You're on, Homes. I hope you're right."

21.

J ack could see the Roswell Police Department ID on his phone as it rang. "What's up, Homes?"

"Good news and bad news, Jack. Good news is that the Southwest flight originated in Norfolk, and our man Gregory Stone was a passenger. Now we know where he lives."

"Or we know he lives nearby somewhere. What if he changed planes in Norfolk?"

"No, I checked on that, too," Homes said. "And the Tennessee Bureau says the driver's license is a fake, just like the one in Pendleton. And there is no insurance agency named Crossman and Blore in Tennessee or anywhere else on the planet. And why is this Memphis guy flying out of Norfolk?"

"Homes, for God's sake. Maybe he was in business there for some other reason. Let's not make too much out of it. So what's the bad news?"

"The FBI's preliminary search has turned up nothing on our Mr. Stone. They're running his photo through all their databases, civilian and military—and through Interpol just for fun. I even ran him on Google just for the hell of it. Nothing. I'm pissed. The guy's got to show up somewhere."

"Homes, why don't you set up one of those phony Internet dating stings using the information we know about him? We can dress you up like a woman—probably a blonde with big boobs. If he bites, we can nail this guy."

Homes was silent for a full minute. "Jack, sometimes you ain't funny. We're getting closer to this guy—you've got to admit that."

"We sure know a lot more than we did yesterday. And I'm convinced now that Mr. Stone and Mr. Kennedy are one and the same guy, even if I can't prove it yet."

"Jesus, Jack, I'm glad you're finally admitting we've got something."

"Homes, I was just thinking. With all this heavy Homeland Security shit we're all dealing with, how can this guy—or anyone—get a phony driver's license that checks out?"

"And you used to be such a good cop, Jackie," Homes said. "Money, baby. Remember that dude a few years back who was caught selling bogus driver's licenses he made up at the state office? He was the assistant director, for God's sake. He had been selling perfect licenses that showed up as legit at airports and everywhere else. If you had enough bucks, this guy could get you what you wanted. Just proves you can outfox the system one way or another. You telling me there isn't a guy like that in a lot of state agencies right now? And even guys outside an agency can copy these things perfectly. It's like counterfeiting money. They can do it, Jack."

"I guess you're right. That still leaves a big problem for me."

Homes sighed. "Jesus, Jack, what is it now?"

"Motive, Homes. What's his fucking motive? I can't figure it."

"Me either. But I've got a couple of other ideas. Call you if I turn up anything else."

22.

ack in Kill Devil Hills, the man who had called himself Stone picked up the Sunday Atlanta newspaper and was caught immediately by the front-page headline: "Abortion May Affect Benjamin Case."

He had previously read of the murder trial of Atlanta psychiatrist Laura Benjamin and made a mental note to keep track of it. But this new information intrigued him. Here was a psychiatrist—one of his least favorite individuals—who had seen fit to take the life of her own father because he had advanced Alzheimer's and been in pain.

Stone had no problem with anyone taking a life—any life—and he did not understand the moral question at issue in the trial. The taking of a human life was simply another one of life's decisions based on personal need—not right or wrong, just need. Like his own growing need—the need that Laura Benjamin must have felt. The fact that there was a law against assisted suicide—*What an absurd description*, he thought—in the state of Georgia was irrelevant to Stone. As he read on, he clutched the newspaper tightly. A thin film of sweat began to show on his forehead. The psychiatrist had apparently broken down on the stand and become hysterical, screaming about her innocence and how much she'd loved her father. The judge had adjourned the trial for the day. The YouTube replay of her breakdown had already received over a half million hits.

He smiled and licked his lips. Here were all the elements he needed, hopefully to make up for the wasted effort in Birmingham. Dr. Benjamin was a distraught woman who had killed someone close to her. She had already gone over the edge once on the witness stand. It would not take much, he thought, to push her to the limit again—and beyond. The fact that she was a psychiatrist made it all the more compelling for Stone. He had read many books on psychiatry and had even been a patient for some time. He had found it easy to outwit that doctor and had considered doing away with him when he'd felt the man might be probing too deeply into Stone's psyche. Unfortunately, he'd had to leave the area quickly before he could deal with the man.

But this Dr. Benjamin situation might—he smiled as he said the old cliché out loud—allow him to kill two birds with one stone. And he was that Stone! He could get revenge on his former doctor through a visit to Dr. Benjamin. Now, his actions with this Benjamin woman would truly be an assisted suicide. He wondered if Benjamin was a drinker or drug abuser. Many doctors were. Of course, if the jury found her guilty, the situation would be resolved, and he would never have the opportunity to correct an old mistake and take advantage of an entirely new situation. He earnestly hoped for an acquittal. Perhaps he would write a letter to the editor, postmarked from Norfolk, pleading for a not-guilty verdict. His elaborate satellite-television listings included a major Atlanta station, WSB, and while he had been recording the trial, he looked forward to watching it live from now on. He also sent an immediate e-mail to one of his private investigators, requesting a detailed personal file on Dr. Laura Benjamin.

23.

J ack rushed up to Laura when the judge adjourned for the day, but as he tried to put his arms around her, she shook her head and pulled away. She was still hysterical and let Barb lead her out of the courtroom.

"It's probably better if I try to calm her down alone, Jack," Barb whispered to him. "I'll keep you informed." The two women headed for the judge's chambers.

The judge was seated when they arrived, with the DA close behind them.

"Sit down, all of you," the judge ordered. "Mr. Glover, I'm going to aim most of these remarks at you. It's patently obvious that you're attempting to focus the jury's minds on the question of abortion. I remind you that abortion has nothing to do with the charges brought against Dr. Benjamin and that the jury must render a verdict solely on the charge of assisted suicide."

"I'm aware of that, Your Honor. But I'm convinced that Dr. Benjamin's actions in aborting her fetus have a direct relation to her actions with regard to her father. They both involve purposely ending lives. The jury has a right to hear how her past actions affected her present actions."

Barb and Laura kept silent. The judge nodded at Glover. "You have every right to present your case as you see fit, Counselor. But I remind you again that Dr. Benjamin is on trial for assisted suicide, not abortion. I also want you to clearly understand that I will emphasize that point when I charge the jury before they deliberate."

"I understand that, Your Honor."

"Barb, do you or your client have any questions?"

"No, Your Honor."

"Then we're finished for the day."

Back in Barb's office, Laura lay down on a sofa, still sniffling but under control. "I'm sorry I lost it there at the end. I know it hurt us."

Barb nodded. "It did have an effect on the jury, Laura. It was unfortunate, but now we just deal with it. And the judge's charge to the jury will help. The problem is that the DA is very good at redirecting the minds of the jury, and right now, all they're thinking about is abortion. And if there is one issue that gets Georgians more excited than assisted suicide, it's abortion."

There was a knock on the door, and one of her paralegals stuck her head in. "Sorry to interrupt, boss, but I thought you would want to see this right away." She walked up to Barb at her desk and handed her a sheet of paper. Barb read it quickly.

"Okay, here's some good news. That domestic-abuse situation with your father was withdrawn by your mother and never adjudicated. There was no injury report and no hospital stay by anyone. No report of alcohol being involved. Sounds like it was maybe a bad argument that was resolved without a further problem. I have the police report here, and I can have someone from the Marlborough Police Department testify. It will help us with the jury if we have an officer read the report."

Laura swung her feet over the sofa and sat up. "I really don't know what that was all about, and I'm glad to hear it's cleared up."

Barb agreed. "Now we deal with the big one. Laura, why did you decide on the abortion?"

"It was the doctor's recommendation but certainly my choice. His name was Hanford or Handler—something like that."

"His recommendation? Based on what?" Barb started to take notes.

"They did a blood test when I came into the clinic. It showed I had type 1 diabetes and high blood pressure. The fetus was six or seven weeks old, and the doctor said there already was a real danger of serious birth defects because of my condition."

"And you had never had any previous indication of diabetes?"

"No, never. Or of high blood pressure. My weight was always under control, and I exercised regularly. I was only twenty-five and still thought I was invincible, of course. The doctor said it wasn't unusual for diabetes to develop in some people later in their lives. And then he said if the pregnancy continued, I might also develop preeclampsia."

Barb nodded. "I remember the term from my own pregnancy. It has something to do with swelling, doesn't it?"

"Yes, swelling in the pregnant woman's feet and toes that usually persists through the entire pregnancy. It could cause the baby to be born early, even brain damaged. And sometimes the mother has seizures or a stroke during labor and delivery."

"How far along did you say your pregnancy was?"

"Six or seven weeks."

"That may help us, too. How long before a fetus is viable?"

"The current literature says twenty-three or twenty-four weeks."

"So your fetus wasn't even close to being developed." Barb hit her fist hard on her desk. "Good God, Laura, why didn't you ever discuss this with me from the very beginning? You have a damn good reason for having the abortion—preventing extreme danger to you and the baby if it came to term. We could have dealt with this so much better if you had told me earlier."

Laura began to cry softly as she nodded agreement. "I know, Barb, but I've carried a lot of shame around over the last ten years because of what happened. I know it was the right decision at the time, but it ended my engagement to a really nice guy I loved, and I've avoided any other permanent relationship because of the fear of another complicated pregnancy. I've never discussed this with anyone—ever."

"I can see where you're coming from. Of course, they started you on insulin right away?"

"Yes, and I'm still on a fairly strict diet, keep track of my blood sugar, and give myself insulin shots as needed."

"Laura, I'm an attorney, not a psychiatrist. But it seems to me you shouldn't be so afraid of relationships because of what's happened."

"I know that, Barb. But no one knows better than a psychiatrist that it takes a long time to get rid of old trauma. I went through a very bad period. I still have a lot of guilty moments."

"Well, this changes things very much for the better in your case." She pressed a button on her intercom. "Sarah, will you come in, please?"

Barb and Laura both gave Sarah information pertaining to her medical procedure and the resolution of the abuse charges. Sarah left to contact witnesses and locate any pertinent documents.

"This still leaves us with some real problems, Laura. Glover will be calling a long list of conservative doctors and clergymen who will testify that they believe abortion is illegal and immoral under any circumstances. He'll be trying to reinforce what he was implying in court today—that you have previously shown a disregard for human life. That's absurd, of course. How all of this will affect the jury is a big unknown and a genuine danger."

"I guess we've known that from the beginning, Barb. I know you'll do your best."

"That I will, my friend. That I will."

24.

"Aubrey, I'm not much on being serious when we get together, but I want to ask you something." Jack had just brought her up to date on the Birmingham suicide he and Homes had investigated. "Should I put my clothes on to hear this?" she said, smiling.

"Uh, that won't be necessary." Jack paused for a moment as he tried to find the right way to say what he'd been thinking about. "Aubrey, there's an opening for a sergeant's position in the Roswell department. You have all the academic requirements and experience for the job. The pay level is excellent. And it's a quick stepping-stone to detective. I think you ought to consider applying for the position."

Aubrey's face was serious, but she didn't say anything.

"There's more. If you get this job, it will be on your own merits. Homes will have nothing to do with it, and neither will I. The captain is a straight shooter, and promotions have been going to officers who work hard and deserve them. There are already a half dozen women in the department in high-level positions. I know your strong feeling about Pendleton and being close to your family and the fact that you've been considering running for sheriff. I still think this would be a great move for you."

Aubrey was still quiet.

"And there's something else. I'll just come out and say it. Whether or not you apply for this job, I'd like you to consider coming to Roswell and moving in with me. I know this would be a big change for both of us, and for the record, I've never asked any other woman to do this. I think you and I have something special going, and I promise that I'll make this as good for you as I already know it will be for me."

"Jack, I don't know what to say."

"I know you'll need some time—a lot of time—to think this over. Whatever you decide, I hope we can still see each other."

Aubrey nodded and took a deep breath. "Can I ask you a technical question?"

"Sure."

"If I move in with you in Roswell, will I have to sleep with Homes, too?"

Jack was glad he could laugh along with her. "I see you're considering all the angles. I think we should look for a new place together."

"Will you hug me, please?" she said. "Just a hug."

"Sure. I need one too."

25

J ack was again in the courtroom for what Barb had told him would probably be close to the last day of testimony. The weekend had given Barb enough time to line up new rebuttal witnesses. Laura had been excused for the moment, and Glover began to parade his witnesses, who condemned abortion on both legal and religious grounds. There were enough heads on the jury nodding in agreement to concern Barb more than she had been. It took a full day of testimony before Glover finished questioning his witnesses. The judge adjourned the trial for the day.

Barb, deciding to save Laura's testimony for last, began the next day with the Marlborough, Massachusetts, police chief, Daryl Corton. The chief was in uniform, of course, and quickly verified that nothing had come of the complaint filed against Laura's father long ago. Barb asked him twice about the withdrawal of the complaint, and that issue seemed resolved. Glover didn't ask him any questions, but Barb knew he was waiting for the abortion witnesses. She had been unable to locate the doctor, now retired, who had treated Laura and recommended the abortion ten years ago. She had found the head of the clinic, a nice-looking older doctor who spoke softly but firmly about the dangers of a pregnancy complicated by diabetes for both the fetus and the mother. He had Laura's original file, which had been well annotated by the doctor she had seen. He showed slides of other diabetic pregnancies that had been brought to term or near term. One case had resulted in the birth of a baby who was badly brain damaged and ultimately died. The mother in the other case had had severe convulsions. The slides and the doctor's testimony had a dramatic effect on the jury.

"So, Doctor, what you're saying is that Dr. Hanson was firm in his recommendation to Dr. Benjamin that she have the abortion."

"Absolutely. His remarks here"—he tapped the file—"are clear. He also consulted with two other doctors on staff, and they agreed with his analysis."

Glover cross-examined the doctor, attempting to get him to admit that not all diabetic pregnancies ended negatively.

"I can't say all of them," the doctor stated, "but I can tell you that over ninety percent of those I'm aware of ended badly for either the mother or the baby or both."

Barb then presented her own string of clergymen and lawyers who gave their opinions about abortion and religion, as well as legal views concerning preterm abortion. The witnesses pointed out that half of the states permitted abortion in one form or another and that even many people who opposed the issue generally did not oppose medical abortions like Laura's to protect the life of the mother.

Glover was on his feet, effectively arguing with the lawyers and doctors. Barb felt she had done a good job, but so had Glover.

She wanted to end the day with her witnesses on the subject of assisted suicide, in an attempt to get the jury's minds back on the reason they were there. She had half a dozen lawyers and doctors who testified that there were genuine arguments for assisted suicide. Then it was Glover's turn again.

Still on the stand was Barb's last witness, Dr. Raymond Clifford, an eloquent spokesperson for assisted suicide who had testified at similar trials all over the country.

Glover was in attack mode from the start. "Dr. Clifford, do you believe that we all have a right to die?"

Clifford smiled. "Well, I wouldn't worry one way or the other. None of us will miss out on the opportunity."

Several members of the jury smiled at this remark, and there was brief laughter in the courtroom.

"This is a serious issue, Doctor, and I'll ask you to treat it that way."

"Don't lecture me about something you know very little about, young man." The doctor looked sternly at the district attorney.

The judge rapped her gavel. "Dr. Clifford, please just respond to Mr. Glover's questions."

"Doctor, do you believe that generally speaking, laws should be obeyed?"

"Generally speaking, yes. The devil, of course, is in the details."

"And isn't it true, Doctor, that the first stipulation in your oath, the Hippocratic oath, is to do no harm?"

"That's well known. In my opinion, allowing a terminal patient to die slowly and painfully would be doing extreme harm."

The DA decided to use a different tack. "Doctor, what's the difference between euthanasia and assisted suicide?"

"To my mind, they are the same. Euthanasia is from the Greek, meaning 'good death.' It is also often called mercy killing."

"And you believe this mercy killing is morally acceptable?"

"I believe in letting the dying determine how and when they die as opposed to artificially keeping them alive at all costs and for no apparent good reason."

The DA smirked and turned toward the jury. "That sounds very noble, Doctor. But what about the law?"

"What about it?"

"Isn't it true, Doctor, that not one of the United States—not one—permits euthanasia?"

"Not exactly. Death with Dignity acts have passed in Washington, Oregon, and Vermont for terminally ill adults whose life expectancy is under six months. Similar laws are being considered in other states. There is also a fairly new Aid in Dying movement gaining traction across the country. Of course, there are many variations in these new laws."

"Our Georgia law specifically forbids this so-called mercy killing you've just described, with no exceptions. So if any person participates in an assisted suicide, they are breaking the law, are they not?"

"I believe there's a higher moral law that should be considered," the doctor replied.

"You mean the one that says, 'Thou shalt not kill'?" Glover smiled at the jury.

The courtroom murmurs began again.

"I think this commandment refers to murder, not to helping someone to end their pain and suffering. I would say that all murder is killing but not all killing is murder."

"It's very convenient of you to reinterpret the Bible to suit your own beliefs, Doctor. Many people in this country, and indeed in the Christian world, would object to different interpretations of that commandment."

"People can interpret it in any way they choose. I've given you mine."

"And do you feel that the Georgia law forbidding assisted suicide can be interpreted in many different ways?"

The doctor smiled, realizing the trap being set by the district attorney. "Mr. Glover, I'll leave the interpretation of law up to the juries and the courts. I simply don't feel it is an offense to lovingly help a sick and dying person in their time of greatest need. I don't think you can legislate morality, and I would suggest that the current Georgia law on this subject is trying to do exactly that."

Barb felt that the DA's exchange with Dr. Clifford was probably a draw and that getting Laura back on the stand before she rested her case was important and crucial. She and Laura had gone over her testimony for hours, and Laura felt she would be able to control herself and answer Barb's questions directly and honestly.

"Dr. Benjamin, it's been quite awhile since you first began your testimony. Please refresh the jury's mind about your relationship with your father."

"My mother died when I was only eight. I came along rather late in their marriage. I have no siblings, and they never expected to have children. So it was just Dad and me together until I went away to college. Dad was both parents to me. I loved him very much."

"Your father was an attorney?"

"Yes, he started out with a small firm in Boston and then went into private practice on his own. He was a brilliant man who genuinely cared for his clients."

"I see. And after you received your psychiatric and medical degrees, you came to Georgia?"

"Yes. I moved to Roswell about six years ago and opened up my practice."

"Your Honor, I'd like to offer exhibits seven through nine, confirming Dr. Benjamin's various degrees."

"So ordered."

"I'd also like to offer—and the district attorney has stipulated to this—exhibits ten through twelve, showing Dr. Benjamin has received the highest certifications and reviews from her professional boards and accrediting organizations."

"They are accepted into the record."

"Now, Dr. Benjamin, when you moved to Roswell, did your father remain in Boston?"

"Yes, for a while. He had been sick for some time. Heart trouble. And the last time I visited him in Boston, I could see he was having problems with his memory, too. So I convinced him to move down here about five years ago."

Barb nodded. "What steps did you take to see to his care at that time?"

"I have friends in the medical community, and he was seen by the top professionals in the area."

"Was your father living with you?"

"He was at first. After a time, he felt his condition was interfering with my personal life and asked me to find him an apartment close to mine. And I did, in the same apartment building."

"What about his continuing medical care?"

"Fortunately, my father had sufficient funds to pay for nursing care at home and, in the last two years, to have someone with him unless I came over to stay with him at night."

"And how often did you stay with your father to care for him?"

"Two or three nights a week."

"And did his health improve?"

"No. Quite the opposite. He was finally diagnosed with Alzheimer's, and his heart condition was inoperable. About six months ago, he began complaining of increasing pain in his abdomen."

"What was that diagnosis?"

Laura paused for a moment, her eyes filling with tears, but she did not cry. "Advanced pancreatic cancer."

"How long did your doctors say he had to live?"

"They said perhaps a year. That was six months ago. They also said that strong, continuing medication would be the only way to control the pain."

"Your Honor, I'd like to introduce defense exhibits eleven through fifteen. These are copies of Dr. Benjamin's father's medical records and his doctors' notes."

"They are accepted into the record."

"I remind the court and the jury that we have already introduced copies of Dr. Benjamin's father's letters to her requesting assisted suicide, as well as her father's living will, health-care proxy, and power of attorney, all giving Dr. Benjamin complete authority as caregiver and decision maker."

"Objection!" Glover was on his feet this time. "None of these documents can give legal permission to Dr. Benjamin to perform an assisted suicide and should not be permitted into the record."

"Mr. Glover, you are overruled. Please continue, Ms. Desmond."

Barb fought to hide a smile. "Now, Dr. Benjamin, you are also a medical doctor in addition to being a doctor of psychiatry?"

"That's correct."

"From a medical perspective, did you notice any recent changes in your father's condition?"

Laura nodded. "Yes. About a year ago, I could see his memory was deteriorating more rapidly, and he began complaining more often about increasing pain."

"You had nurses caring for your father at that time?"

"Yes, and we also had him reevaluated by his doctors."

"What was the outcome of those evaluations?"

"The doctors advised me to hospitalize him for full-time care."

"Were you able to explain this to your father?"

"Yes, during his lucid moments."

"What was his response?"

"He was adamantly opposed to being hospitalized. He also said he did not want his pain medication increased. His lawyer's mind did not like losing focus."

"He was aware of his cancer diagnosis?"

"Yes. His doctors made certain he was aware."

"What happened next?"

"About six months ago, he began to ask me about helping him to pass."

"You mean assisted suicide?"

"Yes."

"What was your response?"

"At first, I refused to discuss it at all. I just said no and that we would explore the possibilities of new procedures and treatments for him."

"Were there any new treatments for his cancer?"

"Nothing that wasn't already part of his care regimen."

"What about his Alzheimer's?"

"No. Nothing new."

"What happened next?"

"One evening about four months ago, his mind seemed extremely clear."

"Objection." Glover was on his feet. "How could Dr. Benjamin know whether her father's mind was clear or not?"

The judge responded quickly. "Since Dr. Benjamin is a medical doctor and had been monitoring her father's care for several years, I'll allow her analysis of his mental capability at that time."

"Thank you, Your Honor," Barb said. "Please continue, Dr. Benjamin."

"On that night, he brought up the subject of assisted suicide again. He had been reading articles on the computer by his bedside."

"Did he know assisted suicide was illegal in Georgia?"

"Yes, he was aware, and I emphasized that to him."

"What happened next?"

"He was afraid—very afraid—that he would have more-serious mental setbacks and not be able to argue for dying on his own terms. He spoke to me as if he were an attorney again, pleading his case."

"What was your response?"

"I just couldn't argue with him. I broke down and said I would do what he wanted." Laura began to cry softly.

"And what did you do then, Doctor?"

"About a week or so later, I dismissed the night nurse and had a brief conversation with Dad. He wasn't as lucid as he had been before, but I asked him several times about the procedure until I was certain he knew what was going to happen. He agreed, and then he"—Laura began to cry openly—"thanked me."

"And what did you do next, Doctor?"

"I administered a dose of morphine sufficient to help him pass. Then I called the police."

"You made no effort to cover up what you had done or even to deny it?"

"No."

"Do you have anything else to say, Doctor?"

"Only that given the same circumstances, I would make the same choice for him. I believe that in these situations, we all deserve a choice."

"Thank you, Doctor."

Glover jumped to his feet. "Dr. Benjamin, you have my deepest sympathies on the death of your father. I'm sure that everyone in this courtroom sympathizes as well. I just have a few additional questions. Do you receive any life insurance from your father's estate as a result of his, um, death?"

"Objection, Your Honor!" Barb shouted out quickly. "Irrelevant and immaterial."

"Dr. Benjamin may answer that question."

Laura paused for a moment. "I think there was a small policy, but I'm not sure—"

Glover interrupted. "Your Honor, I'd like to place prosecution's exhibit five into the record. This would be a life-insurance policy on Daniel Benjamin payable to Dr. Benjamin in the amount of one hundred thousand dollars."

The courtroom murmur increased again. Several jurors looked shocked. The judge wrapped her gavel. "That document is admitted as prosecution exhibit five."

Glover nodded. "Now, Dr. Benjamin, were you fully aware that the Georgia law forbidding so-called assisted suicide, or mercy killing, is quite comprehensive and does not allow any exceptions for advanced or even terminal medical conditions of any kind?"

"Yes, I was aware." Laura bowed her head.

"Final question, Dr. Benjamin. In the remote possibility that you are found not guilty—"

"Objection, Your Honor." Barb's face was livid.

"Mr. Glover, your remarks are out of order and dangerously close to being in contempt—*again*. The jury is directed to ignore your last statement."

"I'll rephrase, Your Honor. Dr. Benjamin, at the conclusion of this trial, if you are ever approached by any person whose medical circumstances are similar to your father's, would you make the same decision concerning his or her life?"

"Objection, Your Honor. Calls for speculation on the part of the witness."

Glover was quick to respond. "Your Honor, Dr. Benjamin is a medical doctor who obviously considered all the elements of her actions in this case, even though, as she has testified, her decision violated her religious beliefs and possibly her Hippocratic oath. The jury deserves to know how she would react in another similar situation."

The judge took her time responding to this point. "I'm going to allow the question. Dr. Benjamin, you may answer."

Laura was caught off guard. Finally, she cleared her throat and said, "My actions concerning my father were done out of love and for no other reason. I can't tell you what I would do in any other circumstance."

With a broad smile, Glover loudly announced, "Your Honor, the state rests its case."

"Redirect, Your Honor." Barb's face was still crimson. "Dr. Benjamin, can you tell us any more about your father's insurance policy?"

Laura nodded. "He told me he had taken it out when I started graduate school. He joked about how he wanted to insure his investment in my education. He never told me the amount, and frankly, I had completely forgotten about it. That was a long time ago."

"I see," Barb said. "Without getting into specific details, can you tell the jury if your psychiatric practice is successful?"

"Yes. I've been very fortunate."

"And are your finances, including your debts, in good condition?"

"Yes. I'm not a millionaire, but I'm comfortable, and I have no debt."

"Thank you, Dr. Benjamin. Your Honor, the defense rests."

"We'll adjourn for today, and I will charge the jury tomorrow morning, beginning at nine o'clock."

The man who had called himself Stone had been watching the trial on television, and he was fascinated with the legal procedure. While Dr. Benjamin was an appealing and even tragic figure, the fact remained that under Georgia law, she had committed murder. And that foul district attorney—was his name Glover?—now, there was a man Stone would have liked to deal with on a personal level. Stone fingered the file concerning Laura Benjamin he had just received from his private investigator. He found it interesting that she was a diabetic. There were ways he could use that when and if they met. But first things first. He had been feeling a growing compulsion to deal with this psychiatrist and had begun making his plans—still tentative, of course, until the final verdict.

27.

losing arguments on both sides were brief and to the point. Barb tried to underscore that Laura had no motive other than love to help her father pass. She spent the bulk of her remarks reminding the jury of the testimony of several defense witnesses who had stressed that in this case, there was a higher moral law that should take precedence over state law and that Dr. Benjamin should not be convicted because of her love for her father.

The district attorney was terse and blunt. Dr. Benjamin had admitted to taking a life before, and her actions against her father proved her propensity for a callous disregard for the sanctity of life. She had broken the Georgia law, plain and simple. This required a penalty of twenty-five years in prison and a cancellation of her license to practice medicine. There was no provision in the law, he said, for any exceptions, including any motivation she might have had for easing her father's pain. Ultimately, she had caused his death, and that was against the law.

The judge's charge to the jury was, of necessity, prolonged and detailed. She emphasized that although testimony had been heard on a number of issues, the jury's ultimate task was to determine if Dr. Benjamin had violated Georgia's law prohibiting assisted suicide, the only charge for which she was on trial. While her past actions could be considered in the determination of guilt or innocence, they should not be the sole or primary factors in the case. She finished her charge by telling the jury she would be available at any time to answer their questions and questions of law. She then dismissed them to the jury room.

Jack hugged Laura as she and Barb began leaving the courtroom.

"Now we wait," he said.

Laura nodded. "Barb, I want to thank you for all you've done. I don't think I could have been defended any better by anyone."

"You're very welcome, Laura. I feel good about the case, but the DA made some excellent points and arguments. And having a half dozen preachers get up there and use the Bible to condemn you—well, it had its effect on the jury. I still think we'll be okay."

"Barb, what's the rule of thumb about how long it takes for a jury decision and whether or not the length of time has a positive or negative outcome?" Jack asked.

"Any rule of thumb is a myth, Jack," she said. "Every jury is different, and I've never found any relation between length of time for a decision and the outcome. I think what we all need to do now is get some rest and hope for the best."

"Jack, will you drive me home?" Laura said. "I don't think I can relax very much if I'm alone."

"Of course."

They drove the thirty-minute trip to Laura's apartment in silence.

"Do you still want me to come inside?"

"Yes, please."

They went into Laura's apartment, and she turned to Jack and began to cry. He held her as her sobs increased and then gradually slowed.

"Let me get you some water or something," he said.

They sat silently on the sofa.

"Jack, I'm going to ask you to do something foolish."

"Ask away. Nothing you could say would be foolish."

"I want you to spend the night, but I don't want—"

Jack nodded. "How about if I camp out here on the sofa? Would that be okay?"

Laura began to cry softly again. "Yes. Yes, that would be fine. I don't know how to thank—"

"Shhh," Jack said, holding her close. "Try to get some rest. I'll be out here if you need me."

The next morning, Jack fixed a small breakfast for the two of them.

"Feel any better?"

Laura smiled. "I don't feel much at all. My feelings have been stretched as far as they'll go. I'm just—well, numb, I guess."

"I've got some things to take care of in the office. I'm going to go to my place first, bring Homes up to date, and then do a little work. If anything happens, call me there."

Laura nodded. "Jack, I'll make this up to you. I'm a little embarrassed about—"

"Don't be. We'll have a lot of time to make up for the past three months."

When his home phone rang, Jack was surprised to see Laura's ID.

"Hey, what's up?"

"Barb just called me. The jury's ready to come back. They want us in court in an hour. I'm scared to death."

"Don't be. Want me to pick you up?"

"Barb's on her way over here now. Why don't you come downtown as soon as you can?"

"I'll pick up Homes and do that. See you soon. And, Laura, this is going to be okay."

The courtroom was filling up quickly when Homes and Jack arrived. They found seats and waited. Finally, the court clerk announced the judge's arrival, and Judge Benson entered the courtroom and seated herself.

"You may bring the jury in. Ladies and gentlemen, while the clerk is gathering the jury, I want to make it clear that I will not stand for any demonstrations or outbursts as the verdict is delivered. I understand that emotions ran high during the trial and that people feel strongly about the issues. Nevertheless, I expect you to act with respect for this court and the process we've gone through over the past few weeks."

There was silence again as the jurors came slowly into the courtroom. Jack kept his eyes on Laura and Barb, who were in deep conversation. Finally, the last juror entered and was seated.

"Ladies and gentlemen of the jury, have you reached a verdict?"

The jury foreperson was a middle-aged woman, a schoolteacher, who had not shown much emotion during the trial. She stood and faced the judge.

"We have, Your Honor."

"May I see the verdict sheet, please?"

The clerk delivered the verdict to the judge, who read it quickly and handed it back to him. He walked slowly back to the foreperson and returned it to her.

"Will the defendant please rise?"

Laura and Barb stood up together.

"The foreperson may read the verdict."

"Your Honor, the jury finds the defendant, Laura Benjamin, not guilty of the charge of second-degree murder."

Despite the judge's earlier remarks, a loud murmur rose from the courtroom.

"Your Honor," the foreperson continued, "we also find that the defendant has violated Georgia Code 16-5-5 concerning assisted suicide. The appropriate licensing board shall revoke the license, certification, registration, or other authorization for Dr. Benjamin to conduct health care of any kind in the state of Georgia, effective immediately."

The foreperson sat down as the noise level in the courtroom rose considerably.

The judge rapped her gavel several times. "The court thanks the jury for its service. Dr. Benjamin, you are free to go. The court is adjourned."

Barb and Laura hugged each other as reporters and cameras surrounded them.

"Jack, does that mean what I think it means?" Homes said.

"Well, we can ask Barb later, but I think it means what the jury said. She's not guilty of murder, but she can't practice medicine any longer in the state of Georgia."

Barb drove Laura home from the courthouse with Jack and Homes close behind. Laura had asked Jack to give her a day or two before they got together. That would give him time to clean up a few cases that were hanging. He also needed to think about his relationship with Laura. She had mentioned before that she would move back to Boston if, for any reason, she couldn't practice any longer in Georgia. That was a reality now, and he knew they would talk about it sometime soon.

"Dr. Benjamin? Laura Benjamin?" The man from Kill Devil Hills, now calling himself Charles D. Starbuck, was using his most pleasant, well-modulated voice.

"Yes, who is this, please?"

"Dr. Benjamin, my name is Dr. Charles Starbuck. I'm on the psychiatric staff at the University of Southern California Keck Hospital, and I also teach at the university. You may be familiar with my work in cognitive neuropsychiatry."

"Your name is familiar, Doctor, but I fear I'm been running behind in my professional reading, and I apologize for not recognizing you." Laura did not recognize the man's name but did not want to appear rude.

"Not at all. Dr. Benjamin, my wife and I will be in Atlanta soon. I'll be meeting with a client for a few days, and I've become familiar with your recent legal proceedings and thought I might contact you. Congratulations, by the way, on your successful verdict. I'm writing a book—my fifth professional work to be published—concerning legal psychiatry. I am placing specific emphasis on psychiatrists who have been personally involved in the courtroom, either through professional testimony or through their own legal circumstances. Your case seems to meet all my specifications, and I would consider it a great courtesy if I could meet with you and interview you for my research."

"Dr. Starbuck, as much as I'd like to be helpful, my recent battle with the legal system still has me quite upset, and I truly don't feel ready to discuss the matter so soon after the acquittal."

Starbuck was prepared for this kind of reply. "I understand that completely, Doctor, and I should tell you that I went through a similar situation with my dear mother several years ago here in California. Of course, there's a much more liberal attitude toward euthanasia out here on the West Coast. Our trials had significant similarities, so I feel safe in saying I know some of what you've been going through. I can schedule a visit to Atlanta whenever you feel you would be ready, and I can promise you that my questions would be sensitive and professional in all respects, as one colleague to another. By the way, you can verify my credentials online on the Keck Hospital site and at the university." Starbuck had, of course, checked the USC website carefully beforehand. He had chosen Starbuck's name because there was no photograph of the man on the faculty website.

Laura considered the man's request. He was, after all, a colleague and fellow psychiatric practitioner. It might do her some good to be able to share her thoughts and feelings with a professional. Talking to Jack and other friends was good, but it wasn't the same.

"Dr. Starbuck, it won't be necessary to verify your credentials. I'm familiar with the professionalism of psychiatrists on the staff at Keck. If you can give me a couple of weeks to get my situation stable here, I'd be glad to speak with you. It sounds as if we can share some similar thoughts and feelings about our parents and their situations. Hold on while I check my calendar." Laura pressed a few numbers on her cell phone. "How does the twenty-first sound to you? That's about three weeks from now."

"That sounds wonderful, Dr. Benjamin. We'll be staying in downtown Atlanta at the Ritz Carlton. Would you be comfortable meeting there? I can rent a private room so we won't be disturbed."

Starbuck did not want to meet at a hotel and was prepared if she chose that option. In that case, he would call her back in a week or two, plead that the hotel did not have a private room available, and ask if she had a suggestion. Either her office or her apartment was his preferred location.

"Oh, that won't be necessary, Dr. Starbuck. I'm closing down my practice and staying away from my office as much as possible. Would it be all right if we met at my apartment? Your wife is certainly welcome as well. And please call me Laura."

Starbuck wanted to laugh out loud at his good fortune. This was another excellent omen.

"You are most kind, Dr. Benj—Laura. That date will be fine. And shall we say late morning—perhaps ten o'clock? And I'm Charles."

"Ten o'clock will be fine, Charles. I look forward to meeting you."

Starbuck turned off his untraceable cell phone and smiled. Reminding himself to order a driver's license and cards with his new identity, he went into his bedroom to lie down and listen again to the Arie Clavin tape.

29.

"was looking forward to meeting you in Charleston," Jack said as he hugged her. "Too much work?"

Aubrey glanced down at her hands and shrugged. "Not exactly. I wanted to talk, and it didn't seem right to drive five or six hours to Charleston. Greenville will have to do."

Jack knew something was wrong. "Sounds like you've made a decision about coming to Roswell."

"Yes, I have. I've made a couple of decisions." She reached out and took his hand. "I guess I'm having the same kind of trouble telling you all this that you had talking to me a few weeks ago."

"Just do the best you can. It'll be okay."

She nodded. "Jack, the job in Roswell sounded great. I checked the website and read more about the department. Nice picture of Homes, by the way."

"I'll tell him you said so."

She looked up at him. "The job wasn't the problem, Jack. The thing I've spent the most time on was our relationship. I'll be honest with you. I've lived with two other men—one in college and one for a few months when I first started this job."

"That doesn't surprise me," Jack said. "It doesn't bother me either."

Aubrey smiled at him. "The boy in college—I should say the man, of course. We had a few criminology courses together. He was sweet, and we were just exploring."

"Aubrey, you don't—"

"Let me say it, Jack. We started seeing each other again a few months ago, right after you first came to Pendleton. He's a lawyer in a small firm in town. Nice parents. We just dated a few times. I didn't think anything would come of it, especially after you and I—well, when we got so close."

Jack sighed and let go of her hand.

"Last week, right out of the blue, he asked me to marry him. I had no idea he felt that way. We talked all night. I told him I had to do some serious thinking and that I'd give him an answer soon. I wanted to talk to you first."

"Sounds like you've made up your mind."

She nodded. "I'm going to tell him yes, Jack. For a lot of reasons. He doesn't make me feel the same way you do, but I'm past the stage where I make important decisions based solely on my feelings. There's got to be family and children and a lifetime close to the things and people I know and love. That's what I want. But I want to know you're going to be okay."

"Aubrey, you've made the right decision, no question. He's your age, and he can give you all the things you mentioned. With me, you'd never know—never be sure. I don't even know if I want kids. Maybe I'm getting to be too old. And the drinking ..."

She took his hand again. "I never considered that, Jack—not the drinking, not your age. It's that small-town thing, I guess, and the fact that I've known him and his people for so long."

Jack stood up. "I think one of the few positive things about being older is that I've been through situations like this before. I have to tell you that it hasn't been with anyone quite like you. So I'll be okay. Don't worry about me." He smiled at her. "Oh, I brought you a present." He handed her a small, brightly wrapped square package. "Please open it now."

She lifted the paper off carefully and looked at the CD: *Bread's Greatest Hits, Featuring "Aubrey."*

"I feel like crying, but I never cry," she said.

"No reason to. Have a great life. I'll never forget you."

30.

Homes burst into their apartment and slammed the door.

"Jack, you got to listen to this. I may have something."

Jack, still brooding about Aubrey, had his head in a football game and was only half listening.

"For Christ's sake, Homes, I'm trying to watch this."

Homes turned off the TV.

"Hey! What the hell?"

"Just listen. A few weeks ago, I decided to write down everything we know about this Mr. Nobody and do some Internet searches."

"Which isn't that much."

"Right. My list had shit like the fact that his victims could be apparent suicides who are connected some way with relatives who may have died the same way. We don't know that he goes after kids, so adults only. He seems to work primarily in the South. He likes to fly into the cities he operates in, at least the two we know about. He's flown out of Norfolk twice, so maybe close to that airport. We figure he's about thirty-five; is tall and slender; has some money; and may like to pose as a lawyer or an insurance guy—that kind of shit."

"Not bad, Homes, but not exactly easy to search for."

"Yeah, tell me about it. So I took some time to put all that into a fairly decent format and sent it out on the Southern Law Enforcement Network. I asked everyone to search the hard facts we know for certain and include apparent suicides, unsolved murders, and even suspicious disappearances in their jurisdictions over the past five years."

"Jesus, how many hits did you get?"

"I got one hundred thirty-three, but some were way off base, so I cut them down to eleven cities or communities, using the best information they could give me and my own good judgment."

"Still sounds like a shot in the dark to me."

Homes nodded. "And it may be, but this case is bugging me, and it gave me something to do."

"So what have you got?"

"Here are my eleven cities: Tallahassee; Charlotte; Jackson, Mississippi; Louisville; Kill Devil Hills, North Carolina—"

"Whoa. Is that a real place?"

"Damn right. On the Carolina coast—the Outer Banks. Some guy from Elizabeth City who was an electronics whiz disappeared there a couple of years ago. The Dare County sheriff from Manteo investigated and talked to the last person they think saw him—a guy who owned a house on the beach where the TV or some shit was being installed. The report says he sells seashells out of the house. They never did find the missing guy or his body."

"Doesn't sound like much. What other cities?"

"Uh, I already said Louisville, so I got Richmond and some smaller towns like Pendleton—Johnson City, Tennessee; Clermont, Florida; Fort Valley, Georgia; Lynchburg, Virginia; and Columbus, Mississippi."

"Anything tie any of those cities together?"

"Not that I can figure out. I marked 'em all on a map that I got in my office. I'll bring it home. Couple of repeat states but nothing that jumps out at me. They're all fairly close to an airport, of course."

Jack thought for a moment. "Homes, I don't mean this to sound like you wasted your time, but how do we know that any of these towns are worth exploring?"

"We don't. This is the longest of long shots."

"So what do we do? How do we decide?"

Homes threw his folder down in disgust. "Beats the shit out of me, Jackie. Maybe biggest town? Smallest town? Funniest name? I don't know."

"That devil town you mentioned—"

"Kill Devil Hills."

"Yeah, is that one close to an airport?"

"Sure is. And that's what makes this one very interesting. What's the only airport we know anything about as far as this guy is concerned?"

"He flies out of Norfolk, Virginia, or at least changes planes there."

"Right. And Kill Devil Hills may sound isolated, but it's only an hour-and-a-half drive to the Norfolk airport."

The two men stared at each other for a moment. "Homes, are you getting the same feeling I'm getting?"

"I've had that same feeling the entire past week, Jack, but it's based on such shitty information I didn't want you making fun of me."

Jack rubbed his hands over his face and through his hair. "I'm not laughing at this one, Homes. This is such a wild fucking stretch that it's probably nothing at all. But it's been so long since we had anything to dig into. At least this gives us something to work on."

"So now that I've almost solved this case for you, where do we go from here?"

"You've already checked the distance to Kill Devil Hills, haven't you?"

"Yep. Ten-hour drive. Of course, we could fly into Norfolk and drive down. Maybe check out the airport a little. Give us the lay of the land. I've already called the sheriff in Manteo. Nice young guy named Ed Martin. He said we could stop by to talk if we wanted."

"I like that better. When do we go?"

"I can take some time off right now. What's your schedule like?"

"Fairly clear. I'm doing surveillance on a couple of divorce cases, and I want to tell Laura why I'll be out of town. Other than that, I'm ready."

"Then let's do this thing, my friend, and maybe find this son of a bitch."

31.

Novak and Homes decided to fly into Norfolk the night before and to try their luck at showing a blown-up photo of Mr. Nobody from his driver's license to the Southwest Airlines counter people and the vendors close to the Southwest gates to see if anyone recognized the man. They had no luck. The same thing happened with the long-term parking office inside the airport. Homes's idea was that one of the surveillance cameras in long term might have picked Mr. Nobody up if he had driven his own car there. Using the two dates they knew he had flown out of Norfolk to Clemson/Pendleton and Birmingham, they looked at several hours of film with no luck. By that time, they were too tired to keep it up. They spent the night at a Hilton close to the airport and got an early wakeup call for the short drive to Manteo and Sheriff Martin.

The sheriff's office reminded Jack of the one in Pendleton. It had the same small-town look and feel. The only difference was that there was an overweight guy in his sixties behind the counter as they walked in. One didn't get lucky and find someone like Aubrey often.

"Officer Kinney and Detective Novak to see Sheriff Martin," Homes said to the man, showing his credentials.

"Sure. Let me tell him you're here." He pressed a button and announced the two visitors, and the sheriff came out to meet them.

"You must have flown in last night to get here this early," the sheriff said.

"That's right. We wanted to do a little checking in the airport but had no luck," Jack said. "We really appreciate you taking the time to hear us out about what we both know may be a long shot at identifying a suspect in a case. I'm Jack Novak."

"No problem at all. And please call me Ed. Homes, I already feel like I know you," he said, shaking hands with Jack. "Now, how can I help?"

"Ed, it's like I told you on the phone," Home said. "We've been looking for a guy for several months now who may be a suspect in a couple of suicides that just look phony to us. One in Pendleton, South Carolina, and the other in Birmingham. He may be involved in others, but those are the only two we know for sure."

The sheriff nodded, sitting down at a computer. "Sounds like you don't have much to go on, but I'm sure we've all had a lot less in other cases. Homes, you said you had a photo and wanted to check a report about a missing person in Kill Devil Hills a couple of years ago."

"Yeah, here's the photo." Homes pulled the blowup of Mr. Nobody's driver's-license photo out of his pocket.

Martin studied the picture and then shook his head. "Don't know him. That doesn't mean anything, because I didn't make the call to Don Dickens's house in Kill Devil when the man disappeared. It was one of my deputies who's no longer with the department."

"Dickens?" Jack was watching the sheriff hit the keys and start his search.

"Yeah, Dickens is the guy who's lived there for a few years. Here's his report from my deputy. He described Dickens as quiet, young, very helpful. Smiled a lot."

Homes and Jack glanced at each other.

"That's a new name for us, Ed, but of course, we never believed either of the names we had was legit."

"Well, I just plugged Dickens's name into the North Carolina driver's-license database. Let's see what we get."

The license popped up in a few seconds.

"Jesus Christ! It's him! It's him!" Homes grabbed on to Jack as the sheriff increased the magnification on the screen. Then Homes held his print against the monitor. "That's him all right, Sheriff. Look at that shitty smile on his face." All three men stared at the screen.

"Nothing phony about the license. He signed up for it through the state driver's-license website. No arrest record. His address checks out. He looks clean."

"He's dirty all right," Homes said, still grinning and patting Jack on the back.

"Guys, I know I don't have to say this, because you know your business. But it seems to me you don't have any proof he did these crimes. Your picture matches his driver's license, and Homes said he can prove the man, under different names, flew out of Norfolk into the Clemson area near Pendleton and then Birmingham, but what if he was just on business?"

It was Jack's turn. "Then why did he use aliases both times and fake driver's licenses and business names that don't exist anyplace in the United States?"

"Good point," the sheriff said. "That wouldn't make any sense unless—"

"Unless what, Sheriff?"

"Well, what if he's working on some secret shit for the government?"

Jack and Homes glanced at each other. "Can you run this Dickens name through the government databases from here?" Homes said, writing down Dickens's local address.

"Sure." The sheriff hit a few more keys. "That'll get anyone who works for the United States government, including the military. If he's some kind of James Bond guy, that will trigger a bunch of red flags in the databases and get us a call from the Feds very quickly. I'll also send his name to the Carolina Department of Justice and ask for a deeper search. This all might take an hour or so. It's a little early for lunch, but how about a late breakfast?"

The three men settled into a local place called the Front Porch Café and ordered coffee. Homes ordered a full breakfast.

"Gentlemen, how about telling me what you'd like me to do? And I'll tell you if I can do it. I agree this is all suspicious as hell, but it's not enough for me to make an arrest. I can put him under surveillance for you if you want."

Jack and Homes both shook their heads. "Sheriff, we need a little time to think this through. We don't want to spook him, and sending one of your guys over there to check on him just might freak him out," Homes said.

Jack accepted another cup of coffee from the waitress. "If you get a hit on the government databases, then we can get the Feds involved, but I just have the feeling there's no record on this guy anywhere. At least not under any name we know about."

"At the same time, I may have a pretty scary murderer in one of my little communities, and that's beginning to bother me," the sheriff said. "How about I give you a week before I check this out any further? Can you deal with that?"

"That's damn decent of you, Sheriff. A week would be great," Jack said.

"Good. Now, let's get back to the office and see if we got any nibbles."

There was nothing positive from Martin's computer search.

"I'm really not surprised, Ed," Jack said. "This guy is a master at hiding any trace of himself."

"We don't need anything else. This is our guy." Homes was still smiling.

"Ed, do you have any objection if we head over to Kill Devil and drive by Dickens's house? We wouldn't contact him or go inside. Just to get a feel for the place."

"No problem with me, boys. Your rental car is clean." The sheriff grinned. "Of course, you damn sure look like city cops, but you ought to be okay."

Jack held out his hand. "Sheriff, I think you've helped us break this case and solve more murders than we really know about. We won't forget it."

"Glad to be of service, gents. When we get this thing cleaned up, why don't the two of you come back, and we'll do some deep-sea fishing? Anytime you like."

"We'll do that, Ed, and thanks again." Homes shook his hand, and he and Jack left the office and got into their car.

Homes pounded Jack on the shoulder. "We've got this son of a bitch, Jack. We've got his ass! Let's go take him down right now!"

"I know you're right, Homes, but let's not blow it. Let's drive by his address nice and easy, talk it through, and then get back to Roswell and make a plan."

During the twenty-minute ride from Manteo to Kill Devil Hills, Jack and Homes traded various scenarios and how they would react to them.

"What if the fucker is in his front yard when we drive by, Jack?"

"We ignore him and keep driving. After all, he's never seen us. No reason he would notice."

"I guess so. What if we don't see his car? Can we stop and check out the house?"

"Not a good idea, Homes. If he has a car, it's probably around back, and he'd notice us if we went nosing around."

"This is frustrating as hell, Jack. If we were in Roswell, I'd know how to handle it—wait till nightfall and just go grab his ass and take care of him. Like we did with those Cambodian fuckers that almost finished you."

"But we're not in Roswell, buddy. Hey, check the address. I think we're coming up on the place."

Dickens's home was a small ranch-style house weather beaten to the point that they couldn't tell the original color. An old, worn sign outside the carport said The Devil's Smile—Beach Jewelry.

"Homes, maybe I'm getting paranoid, but has it ever struck you that this guy is playing games with us? I mean, with everybody?"

"How do you mean?"

"Take his living in Kill Devil Hills and calling his so-called business the Devil's Smile. Even his name—Dickens. Like he's kidding us about who and what he really is."

"Jesus, Jack. I never thought of it that way. Cut that shit out, will you? I'm already spooked enough as it is."

There was no sign of movement in the house or a car. There were no other homes as far as they could see up and down the highway as they drove past.

"I'm going to drive a mile or two down the road and then turn back. I'll take another slow roll past the house and then head back to the airport. We're a little early, but we can spend that time talking over what we need to do next."

Homes sighed. "Okay with me, I guess. I'd still like to bust in his place, wrap him up, and make him disappear."

"I know what you mean. Here's the house. See if you can spot anything."

"Jesus, it's right on the friggin' ocean, isn't it?" Homes said. "Must be hell out here in a storm. Hey, I didn't mean to say *hell*. I just meant—"

"I know what you meant. And you're right. Let's get out of here before we decide to do something foolish." Jack stepped on the gas.

32.

The man now calling himself Charles Starbuck woke suddenly in the dark. He sensed something was wrong. Starbuck couldn't recall ever being afraid. Perhaps he'd been afraid when he was a child and his parents had come into his room and done grotesque things to him or when they had tied him up in a chair and forced him to watch them performing their disgusting sex acts.

Tonight it was a different feeling, and he had experienced it only once before. Several years ago, he had visited a young widow in Columbus, Mississippi, who had accidentally run over her child playing in the driveway. He had been successful in prompting her to relive the entire experience, and she'd screamed, cried, and attempted to take her own life. In the end, he'd allowed her to do that after supplying her with the necessary tools. The recording he had made at that time was remarkable, and he still listened to it occasionally.

The woman's death had attracted a great deal of attention in the town, and someone—he never knew who—had begun trying to find him. He could feel it. It had prompted him to move to Kill Devil Hills and establish a new identity. Now he could feel it again.

Starbuck sat up in his bed and tried to identify the source. The only time in his five or six years in the Hills when he had ever had any kind of encounter with law enforcement had involved the young man who'd installed his communications equipment. Perhaps Starbuck had quizzed the man too intensely about making certain everything was well concealed. That had prompted a lot of questions, and ultimately, Starbuck had had to eliminate him. A week or so later, a county deputy had come by, looking for the man. Evidently, his mother had told some law-enforcement people that Starbuck's job was the last one her son had gone out on. Starbuck had been prepared for the sheriff's visit and gone out of his way to be helpful.

He'd shown the deputy through the house and outside as well. Of course, there had been no trace of the man, and Starbuck had carefully hidden his car. Late the night of his visit, Starbuck had driven the dead man and his vehicle several miles from his home and run the car into Dismal Swamp—he loved the name—near the Nags Head Woods Preserve, where it had gradually sunk into the slime. He'd enjoyed watching it disappear slowly into the ooze. The locals all said the fourteen-hundred-acre swamp was bottomless. But even if it wasn't and the car was recovered, there would be no evidence implicating Starbuck.

There was another of Starbuck's bodies in the swamp too—a teenage girl who had come by the house one day to look at his seashells. She had just lost her mother to cancer, had been alone, and had been hitchhiking. High on some kind of drug, she'd spent the day crying her heart out to Starbuck, who, fortunately, had been able to turn on a tape recorder in his living room to capture all of the girl's laments. He'd had to dispose of her quickly, although he had been able to experiment with her in interesting ways with a wide variety of his drugs and other tools. There had been no repercussions from that incident either.

Starbuck knew that what he was feeling was instinctual. He had not seen any increased law-enforcement activity around his home or in the general area. He had not been followed and had not had any close encounters with anyone on his trips. He was certain the private investigators he used—never the same one twice—to compile background information on his victims were not checking up on him. If he'd had even the slightest hint of their involvement, he would have eliminated them. And the various individuals who prepared his identities—again, he used each one only once—were more interested in the huge sums of money he paid for their services than in exposing him. Besides, none of them knew his real name or location.

No, this feeling was pure instinct, and Starbuck had learned to trust his instincts and move quickly to protect himself. He would leave the Kill Devil Hills home soon—and his trip to Roswell to see Dr. Laura Benjamin was an excellent time to make it happen. He would leave the house exactly as it was, with nothing left to trace. It would be another unsolvable mystery. Perhaps they would say he'd drowned in the ocean during a storm or from a strong tidal wave. The idea pleased Starbuck. He would start preparing in the morning. With that decision made, he slept soundly through the rest of the night.

33

"**S**orry this has taken so long, Jack." Laura still looked tired a week after the trial.

"I think you need a real vacation. Why don't we get out of here for a week or so? Go someplace warm. Maybe the Caribbean or Mexico. Soak up some sun."

Laura smiled. "That sounds awfully good. I'm obligated to find other psychiatrists for my patients before I do anything else. The state board tells me I have ninety days to do that before I completely shut down my practice. I can't even have any more sessions with anyone. I've hired an intern to help put records together when my patients agree to be transferred. Some of them don't want anyone else." She stopped, and tears came to her eyes. "Dammit. I told myself no more crying."

"It's okay. Cry if you need to. So what happens after your office is shut down?"

"Well, I've made a decision. I can't practice anywhere in the state of Georgia. Barb has suggested we appeal that portion of the verdict, and I might have decided to do that, but the idea of going through more legal manipulations right now is pretty much unbearable. I thought about teaching, too, and I have a few good friends at Mercer, Morehouse, and UGA who have asked me to send résumés. The problem is, I really loved practicing, and I was good at it. I think I helped quite a few people." She looked up at Jack. "I'm going to move back to Boston, Jack, and form a partnership with two friends from medical school."

"As much as I hate to hear you say it, I know it's the best thing for you." He leaned toward her, but she turned away.

"Jack, I'm not ready for—I'm not ready yet. I'm sorry."

He nodded and reached out for her hand.

"You're a good guy, Jack. How have you been doing?"

"You mean with the drinking? Okay. I go to meetings when I can. Ought to do more. Of course, I have Homes checking on me all the time. What did you call it—assessing me? He's funny about it, but it helps to keep me straight."

"And that case you were working on?"

"The short story is that Homes and I finally located the man we think is responsible for several murders. Since we still couldn't prove what we feel we know, our plan was to, well, kidnap him and take care of the problem ourselves."

"You mean—"

"Yes. We couldn't figure out any other way, and we think the murders we know about are only the tip of this guy's iceberg. Neither Homes nor I could stand the idea of just letting him loose."

Laura shook her head slowly. "I know this will sound strange coming from a woman who has just been on trial for taking her own father's life, but I have to say I'm a little stunned that you would consider, well, doing away with a person you don't really know. I mean, what if you're wrong? And why not bring in the police?"

"Laura, we've spent months tracking this man and identifying him. Homes and I have a lot of years dealing with murderers of all kinds. I can't explain how, but we get feelings about these kinds of things—most cops do—so we felt pretty confident about our decision. And we did bring in the police when we located him. Now I'm waiting to hear from the sheriff we worked with."

"Jack, I didn't mean to question your judgment. I guess I've just had enough discussion of death lately, and I'm trying to avoid any mention of it."

"I can't defend what Homes and I decided. We could argue the morality issues both ways, I know. I still feel this was a good decision. Unless the sheriff contacts us with some new information, we're just waiting for the next shoe to drop—reading in the paper about some questionable suicide or a missing person and wondering if he's back in his game again."

34

Jack didn't recognize the area code on the caller ID and figured it was a cold sales call.

"Jack, it's Ed Martin in Manteo."

"Sheriff, good to hear your voice. How are things?"

"Things are fine. But I may have bad news for you about our friend Mr. Dickens."

"Don't tell me you had to shoot him. Homes and I want that pleasure ourselves."

The sheriff chuckled. "No, nothing like that. He's just disappeared."

"What?"

"That's right. Completely gone. No trace of him anywhere. I waited a week or so to check on him, as I told you. One of my guys drove by the house and didn't notice anything. He followed up every day for five days and then decided to stop and check inside the house. If Dickens was there, he was going to ask him if he'd seen a motorcycle gang we've had in the area lately. Dickens wasn't home. Nothing in the house had been removed. All his clothing and personal items were still there. At first, we thought he was out of town, but he would normally have taken some clothing and other things with him. And here's the kicker."

"What's that?"

"There were no prints in the house, Jack. Not a one. We even checked the switch on an electric razor in the bathroom and on his TV remote. Nothing in any room, not even on any windows. It was a total blank."

"Maybe the son of a bitch wore gloves all the time."

"Had to be doing something," the sheriff said.

"I remember he doesn't have what you would call neighbors close by, but did you get anything from people in the area?"

"Nothing at all. It's like he never lived there. He made no contact with any local Realtors about selling the place. We can't figure it. Maybe he drowned."

"Not that bastard. He's too smart. He's alive all right. Something tipped him off. He's just moved his location. We'll read about a suicide soon or an unsolved murder and wonder if it's him. Damn, I wish Homes and I had gone after him."

"Well, I'm glad you didn't. I would have had to throw both your asses in the county jail, and it ain't pretty. The food is pure shit." The sheriff started laughing.

"I know you'll call me if something else turns up, Ed. Thanks for keeping me informed."

"Glad to be of service. Tell Homes I said hello."

35.

"**D**ammit, Jack. I knew we should have grabbed his ass and taken him out ourselves."

"Sheriff Martin would have known right away it was us, Homes."

"Who gives a shit? He couldn't prove it, just like we can't prove this Dickens guy is guilty. Now the fucker has disappeared."

Jack nodded. "I know you're right. I guess we'll just have to keep on looking."

Homes studied his friend's face. "Something else has been on your mind lately, Jackie. What's happening with you?"

Jack sighed. "I haven't told you about Aubrey."

"Aubrey—what the hell kind of name is that?"

"It's a nice name—a good name."

"Don't tell me it's from one of those damn Bobby Darin songs."

"No, she's someone I met in Pendleton."

"Oh, the so-called law-enforcement personnel you were working with late into the night?"

"Yeah. She's actually a local deputy with the Pendleton sheriff. Sweet kid."

Homes laughed. "Kid? Kid? Jesus Christ, Jack, please tell me she was out of high school."

Jack smiled. "She's twenty-five and very smart."

"Oh, sure. Twenty-five. So that makes you *only* twenty years older than she is. A great sign of maturity, Jack. You're almost behaving like a grown-up."

"You can kiss my ass, you old pervert," Jack said, heaving a pillow at Homes.

"So what's the problem with this Abbie?"

"It's Aubrey. We were getting pretty close. A couple of weeks ago, I asked her to think about applying for a job here in the department."

"Is she good enough—I mean as a cop?"

"You bet your wrinkled ass she's good enough. We'd be lucky to get her." Jack paused and scratched his head. "I also asked her to move in with me."

"You did *what*?"

"Yeah, that's a first for me."

"What did she say?"

"She asked me if she'd have to sleep with you when she moved in."

Homes laughed so loudly that the cat jumped off the sofa and ran into the bedroom. "Of course you told her yes!"

"I did no such thing."

"Jack, buddy, it's always been share and share alike with us, hasn't it? Haven't I given you half of all my beer?"

"I don't drink beer anymore."

"Well, you used to drink half a case a night. I shared that with you."

"Homes, beer and women are not the same."

"But there are similarities. We have talked about this before. They are both intoxicating, for instance."

"You heard that on some TV show."

"Yeah, I think it was one of those zombie movies."

"Homes, you are a strange man."

Homes ignored his friend. "Look, judging by the incredible women you've been involved with in the past, I would have paid money to have this little honey move in with us. Like that Carol Chambers chick who lived in Camelot—the one with the Cambodian diamonds. I would have paid half my pension for a night with her."

Jack shook his head. "You know, you really are an old pervert. That woman would have driven you nuts. Besides, Aubrey turned me down."

"How come?"

"Two things. She wants to stay in Pendleton. It's her hometown, and she knows everyone there. Eventually run for sheriff. And one other thing."

"Yeah, what?"

"Some guy asked her to marry him."

Homes thought for a moment. "Well, what's the problem? We could have found room for him in the apartment, too."

Two more pillows hit Homes before he could duck.

"On a serious note, Jack, how are you handling this? I mean, really?"

"So far, so good."

"You don't want a drink?"

"Homes, I want a drink all the time, every day, every minute."

"But you aren't drinking?"

"No. At least not for the time being."

"I think you just need to get laid, my friend." Homes walked to the kitchen and opened another beer. "You told me you were going over to see Laura. How did that work out?"

"Not so good. She's moving back to Boston and joining a practice with a couple of friends she knew in med school."

"I thought she was thinking about teaching around here somewhere?"

"She was. She said she finally came to the conclusion that a complete life change would be the right thing for her. Get away from everything that reminded her of her father, the trial—all of that."

Homes sat back down next to his friend. "So where does that leave you?"

Jack tried to smile. "It leaves me zero for two this month in the women department. Laura and I like each other, and we were working on a great relationship. But all of the shit that happened just changed everything—at least for her."

"So you're available again," Homes said, slapping his friend on the back.

"I guess you could say that. You got any old girlfriends you can send my way?"

"Hey, you're the guy with the collection of old girlfriends, most of whom are not that old. Time to get out the little black book, my friend. Or I can fix you up with a nice little cutie on the Russian-bride Internet site."

"Thanks, but I have enough trouble with women who speak English. I think I'll give it a rest for a while. Laura will be leaving in another week or so, and I want to stop by one last time to give her a present—a pearl necklace I found."

"Well, give her my best. And you're still okay?"

"Yes. I'm a little surprised at myself after freaking out over women leaving me in the past. But so far, so good."

"Jack, I'm telling you what you really need is some noncommittal sex."

"That's what I love about you, Homes. Simple solutions for complex problems."

"Hey, Jack, *simple* is my middle name."

"You can say that again." This time, it was Jack who ducked two pillows.

S tarbuck was uncertain what to expect when he visited Laura
Benjamin. Would she emotionally collapse quickly and give
him what he badly needed—expressions of pain and anguish,
begging, screaming? He didn't want a repeat of the fiasco in Birmingham
with Carson Weber. Having to use his paralyzing drug Neuromaxim
was usually a last resort for Starbuck. Nevertheless, he always came
prepared with a vial and syringe of the drug, as well as others.

Reading over his notes, he reflected again on two things. Dr. Benjamin
was a type 1 diabetic and required periodic insulin injections. An acute
overdose of insulin would rapidly bring about seizures, unconsciousness,
and death. He could film and record all of that with his cell phone, of
course. That method had proven satisfactory several times in the past.
He recalled with a smile an instance of a diabetic nurse in Perry, Florida,
whose convulsions and strangling sounds from his injection had lasted
for an unexpectedly long time. He had transferred that recording to a
disk, and he reminded himself to play it again soon after he relocated.
The downside of using insulin was that it required refrigeration or at
least a cooling device of some kind. Starbuck had found a small battery-
operated thermoelectric cooler module online that fit neatly into his
briefcase and would keep a vial of insulin cool for several hours. Any
medical autopsy would invariably state that the person had accidentally
or purposefully overdosed. It made no difference to him. Using insulin
had its advantages and was a distinct possibility.

The method that particularly appealed to him in Laura Benjamin's
case, however, was one he had used before, the same technique she
had used to end her father's life: an overdose of morphine. That drug

didn't require refrigeration, and he was generally pleased with the results. Through trial and error, he had found that he could combine Neuromaxim and morphine, using the former drug first to cause paralysis, and then, when his patient regained motor function, inject enough morphine to bring about lethargy and incoherence. He had learned that with a patient in that condition, he could still inflict extreme pain on the person and prolong the agony he or she experienced.

The Neuromaxim seemed to lessen the painkilling effects of the morphine, which was satisfying. And when he felt the patient's response to pain was deteriorating, an increased dose of morphine would end it all. The one disadvantage was that this combined drug use required more time than he usually felt comfortable allowing himself. He would have to assess the situation with Laura Benjamin to see which method proved most beneficial to his own needs. Of course, there was also the irony factor—killing Benjamin the same way she had killed her father. Starbuck enjoyed irony almost as much as he enjoyed omens. He packed vials and syringes of each drug in his briefcase, checked his appearance once more in the bathroom mirror, and then left the Ritz Carlton in Buckhead for the short drive to Roswell.

Good morning, Dr. Benjamin. I'm Charles Starbuck." His smile well in place, he stood at the doorway to Laura's apartment with his briefcase, having turned his tape recorder on as he left his car.

Laura held out her hand and was surprised to find Starbuck wearing rubber gloves.

"Please forgive the gloves, Laura. I have a minor dermatitis problem and don't want to pass on any possible germs." *Always put them at ease.*

"That's quite all right, Charles. Please come in."

Starbuck walked into the apartment and glanced around quickly. "What a lovely home you have, Laura."

"Thank you. Of course, it won't be mine for long. As soon as my practice is completely closed, I'll be leaving to join some colleagues in Boston."

Starbuck put on his best sympathetic expression. "That was a most unfortunate result of your trial, Laura, and a travesty of justice in Georgia, I'm afraid. Boston will be honored to have you."

"You're kind to say that. Please sit down." She gestured at the sofa. "Would you like some coffee or a soft drink?"

"Why, yes, please. Some coffee would be fine."

Starbuck placed his briefcase on the coffee table and leaned back into the comfortable sofa. "I should apologize for my wife not being here. I'm afraid the shopping available in Atlanta captured her attention completely. And I must admit she is often bored by my shop talk with colleagues." He smiled at Laura in the kitchen. *Thinking I'm married will further disarm her.*

"The shopping has distracted me too," she said, walking back into the living room with a tray and coffee essentials. She placed them on the small table in front of Starbuck and sat across from him.

"Laura, I know your time is important, and I promise not to take up too much of it. I have to tell you that the most dramatic part of your trial I watched on television was the moment you stood up and cried out your love for your father and what you did to take away his pain. You didn't care about any negative results from the jury. I felt a special bond with you then. Could you—would you—go over those moments for me?"

Laura cleared her throat and thought about Starbuck's request. She had tried not to mentally rerun scenes from the trial but had not been successful. Nightmares had become frequent, and she had not had a full night's sleep in the six weeks since the trial ended.

"I know this is difficult for you, Laura," Starbuck added. "As a professional colleague, I remind you that talking through a stress situation can help relieve it and partially ease the discomfort you may still be experiencing." *Always be helpful and understanding.*

"I know you're right, Charles, and I think it's a good idea to try. I'll apologize in advance if I become emotional and lose my composure."

Starbuck was quick to respond and was genuinely sincere. "Oh, please don't hold back, Laura. The more emotion you feel and can express, the better off you will be. Just let it all out, as I'm sure you've told your own patients many times."

Laura began telling Starbuck about conversations she had had with her father leading up to the night she had taken care of him. Starbuck tried to look interested.

He attempted to delicately bring her back to the moments of crisis in the trial—the newspaper story about her father's arrest for abuse, the abortion, the years she had taken care of her father, and his asking her to end his life. While she began crying at several points, she was not losing full control, as he had hoped she would.

"I'm sorry, Charles. Can we take a break for a while?"

"Of course, Laura. I apologize if my questions caused you any upset." Starbuck glanced at his watch. He was getting nowhere just by questioning her. He would have to rely on one of his alternate plans—using drugs and inflicting pain to get what he wanted.

"I wonder if we could have more coffee," he said.

"Of course. I could stand a refill myself.

With Laura in the kitchen, he opened his briefcase and withdrew a photograph of a smiling older woman.

As she came back into the living room, Starbuck said, "Laura, I thought you might like to see a picture of my mother, Constance Starbuck." He handed her the photo. Starbuck had found it at a garage sale in Johnson City, Tennessee, during another of his visits.

"How sweet," Laura said, holding the picture. "How old was she when she—"

"When she passed? Only fifty-nine, but the cancer had ravaged her body so completely that she looked a great deal older. She had many friends in the Los Angeles area near the university, and several of them testified at my trial that they had overheard her begging me to release her from the pain." Starbuck could almost feel tears starting to form in his eyes. Laura handed the photo back to him.

"Laura, during our conversation, I feel we've already become close because of what we've shared about our parents and the sacrifices we've had to make as a result of our decisions. I wonder—I know this is a big thing to ask, but I wonder if you would share a photograph of your father with me? I would consider publishing it in my book, along with those of several other colleagues who have had experiences similar to ours. You could write a tribute to him that would accompany his picture. And if you prefer not to publish it, just seeing his face this morning would mean a great deal to me." Starbuck wiped his eyes with a handkerchief.

Laura was touched. Standing up, she said, "Charles, I don't know about publishing his photo, but let me get one now to show you, and we can decide later on if it belongs in your book."

As she left the room, Starbuck took out a vial of Neuromaxim and added it to Laura's coffee. It was time to begin what he had come for.

Laura returned with the photograph of her father, handed it to Starbuck, seated herself, and took a long sip of coffee.

"He's a good-looking man, Laura," Starbuck said. "You can see the integrity in his face."

"Yes. He was known for that integrity as an attorney." She took another sip and placed her cup on its saucer, putting a hand to her face. "I feel so ..." As she slumped forward, Starbuck caught her and moved her back to a sitting position in her chair. As was usual with the drug, her eyes remained wide open, but she could not speak or move.

"Laura, I'm going to have to speed up our little visit. You see, what I need from you is a stronger expression of emotion—much stronger. Unfortunately for you, the only way I can get that is to use some drugs and then a few of these." He removed a roll of leather-wrapped stainless-steel dental instruments and spread them on the coffee table.

"You see, the drug I've just given you will keep you quiet and immobile temporarily. In a moment, as the drug begins to wear off and you are able to move, I'm going to administer a few milligrams of morphine. Then I'll begin using these interesting dental tools on you in places which will cause the most pain. I would apologize, but you see, this is why I am here. This is what I need." He watched her eyes widen with fear, tears forming. He glanced at his watch and then checked to see if she was able to move. He noticed a small twitch of a finger and then a similar reaction from a foot. It was time.

He filled a syringe with the precise amount of morphine and leaned over her. "I'm always amused in movies when I see some medical person use an alcohol rub before administering an injection. There's no point in using one here, is there, Laura? You won't be needing any germ protection." He injected her and watched her reactions. Her hands slowly opened and closed, as did her eyes. She opened her mouth but wasn't able to speak, at least not yet.

"Soon, you'll want to start screaming, Laura." He smiled at her and patted her head. "I'll want you to scream too. Not too loudly, mind you. Just enough for me to record you. Let's try this first."

He reached over to the row of dental instruments and found a small battery-powered drill. "Laura, did you know that the nerves in your mouth, just under the gums, are some of the most sensitive in your body? Here—let me show you." He turned on the drill and held up her head. Her mouth fell open.

38.

J ack left his apartment and decided to stop by the office before going over to Laura's place. He wanted to check his messages and add a few notes to a case he was closing out. The two locations were only a few blocks away. As he sat at his desk, he glanced at the safe up against one of the walls. He hadn't opened it in a while but knew it contained a fine bottle of single-malt scotch—eighteen-year-old Highland Park—and his weapon, of course, a Glock 17 Gen4. He was fond of both but didn't need either at the moment. In fact, he hadn't had to use his weapon since shooting that Cambodian killer about a year ago. He turned his attention back to his computer and finished up his remarks. Then he left the office, got into his car, and headed for Laura's.

Homes was leaving the apartment, when he noticed Jack's gift for Laura sitting on the foyer table they used for their mail. Chuckling, he picked it up, checked his uniform in the mirror, and headed out the door. "I think I'll drop by Laura's and interrupt whatever the hell they're doing. I've embarrassed Jack every other way—might as well take a shot at this."

39.

tarbuck was a little disappointed. Laura had shown some response
to his dental treatments but not as much as he had anticipated
and hoped for. "Perhaps too much morphine," he said to himself.
Then he noticed that Laura had begun to try to raise her arm.

He slapped her hard across the face and saw her eyes roll back. *That would make a good picture,* he thought, and he paused to pick up his cell phone. "Don't worry, my dear. This will be over soon. I do want to hear you scream once or twice. Remember, not too loudly, mind you. Wouldn't want to disturb the neighbors."

He estimated a slightly smaller dose in a syringe, injected her, and then casually looked over his assortment of tools and chose a flat-edged implement he had used before for prying up gums to expose the nerves. The knock on the door was only a minor distraction. He had planned for this kind of disturbance. An unexpected guest might mean even more entertainment. He picked up a syringe filled with Neuromaxim and walked toward the door.

Homes saw Jack's car outside Laura's apartment building and pulled into the space beside it. He picked up the present on the seat next to him, checked his appearance again in the rearview mirror, and headed inside the building. He pressed the elevator button and smiled to himself as he thought about interrupting Jack and his girlfriend.

When Starbuck opened the door, he saw a tall, handsome man with a stunned expression on his face. He had never seen him before and was shocked to hear the man yell out, "Dickens!" Starbuck took a step back into the apartment and watched the man lunge toward him. He had always thought himself invincible and was not afraid. As Jack reached out to grab him, Starbuck plunged the syringe filled with Neuromaxim into the side of Jack's neck. Jack was able to get his hands around Starbuck's throat and begin to squeeze, when the drug took effect, and he dropped to the floor, unable to move.

Starbuck, still wondering how this stranger knew his Kill Devil Hills name, blinked once and decided to finish his work with Laura quickly and then dispose of them both with overdoses of morphine. He walked back over to Laura and checked her pulse and eyes.

"I'm sorry, my dear, but our visit must come to an end. I don't know who your friend here is, or even if he is a friend, but when the police arrive, they may work out one of their idiotic scenarios where a lover's quarrel ensued and you took each other's lives." He walked over to Jack's body, picked up the syringe on the floor, and then went back to his briefcase for his second syringe. Starbuck knew that about two hundred milligrams of morphine could cause death in most people who were not already drug addicted. He filled each syringe with five hundred milligrams, knowing that dosage would cause death in less than a minute. He walked back over to Jack's body and knelt down to give him the injection, when he noticed that the apartment door was not fully closed. *Must be more cautious.* Starbuck stood up and walked toward the door, syringe in hand.

At that moment, another man pushed open the door. Their eyes met, and the man appeared to be shocked. He shouted out the same name Starbuck had heard from the first stranger: "Dickens!" This man, in a police uniform, was older and more rugged appearing. *This is not a good omen,* Starbuck thought. Unafraid, he advanced toward him with his syringe.

"Hold it right there, Dickens, or whatever the fuck your real name is!" Homes shouted as he drew his gun. "Drop whatever that shit is in your hand, and get down on the ground."

How absurd, Starbuck thought as he continued to move toward the police officer. Homes dropped to one knee, took aim, and fired. The last thing Starbuck ever saw was this strange man smiling at him as the bullet entered just below his left eye. Of course, he never felt the second shot, which pierced his heart.

Homes checked Dickens's body to make certain he was gone. He grabbed Jack's wrist and was surprised to find a strong pulse. At first, he'd thought his friend was probably dead. Turning to Laura, he found her pulse much weaker. It looked as if several of her teeth had been crushed or broken, and blood was streaming from her mouth. She was incoherent. Homes called in the homicide team and asked for an ambulance. In a minute, he could hear the sirens in the distance.

40.

J ack was coming out of the Neuromaxim as they slid him into one of the ambulances. Homes was standing beside him. "Laura," Jack muttered to his friend.

"The docs say she'll be okay. They've just taken her to Northside. That's where you're headed too. They don't know what Dickens shot you full of, and they want to be certain you're okay."

"Feel better ..."

"Yeah, and you're starting to look better, but like I say, they want to check you out. I'm riding with you. Want to make sure you don't drink any alcohol in the ambulance." He smiled at Jack.

"Dickens," Jack managed to mumble.

"Deader than an old pile of shit, which is what he was. Too bad you couldn't see him go down." He smiled at Jack again.

41

T he hospital released Jack the next day. He and Homes were back in their apartment.

"So he never drew a weapon on you?"

"Nope. Didn't have any weapon. Just had this needle full of enough dope to kill ten horses. He was walking toward me with this puzzled look on his face. Guess he thought he'd just walk right up to me and stick that thing in my ass and kill me." Homes took another swallow of beer. "Guess he didn't know how much I hate shots."

"How many times did you fire?"

"Twice. One in the eye, one in the heart."

"Just like you used to preach to me."

"Yeah. What a weird fucker. That reminds me—how many times is it now that I've saved your sorry ass?"

"I've lost count. So who is Dickens really?"

"They still don't know. They ran his prints through every database on the planet and came up with nothing. He was wearing rubber gloves, by the way."

"Any ID on him?"

"Just a phony Charles Starbuck license with an address in Los Angeles. He had some cards in his wallet that said he was a professor at USC. I called out there and talked to the real Starbuck. He doesn't know who Dickens is or what the fuck is going on."

"Laura?"

"They can't get too much out of her. Her mouth is really messed up, and it's hard for her to talk. She wrote a few answers down on a pad. A dentist has been visiting her in the hospital, trying to put her mouth back together. Jack, that bastard had a briefcase full of shit he used to torture Laura and probably quite a few others. And a tape recorder— the asshole had a tape recorder running all the time, along with taking pictures on his throwaway phone. The worst thing was that packet of dental tools that he—"

"Homes, I'd rather not hear about that, please."

"Sure. Sorry. Makes you wonder if there's a whole collection of that shit—recordings and photos—lying around somewhere."

"There are so many things I can't figure out. How did he know about us and Laura? How did he make the connection? And I still can't figure his motive."

Homes shook his head. "Don't think we'll ever know, Jackie. He must have spotted us somehow in Kill Devil. That made him pull out. But how he found out where we were from and put us together with Laura—beats the shit out of me. As for motive, maybe there is no motive. Maybe he's just nuts." Homes took another long swallow of beer. "Speaking of nuts, how you feeling?"

"Other than a little headache, I'm feeling fine. What was that stuff he stuck me with?"

"They don't know that either. It knocks you out in about thirty seconds, lasts for maybe ten, fifteen minutes, and then disappears. There's no sign of it in your blood anymore. It's driving my lab guys nuts. The central FBI lab in DC is flying in here tomorrow to get a sample. Just be glad he didn't stick you full of morphine, or you'd be sitting on a cloud, listening to Bobby Darin in person."

Jack forced a smile. "You have such a delicate way with words. Homes, I know that you've caught a bunch of badasses in the past, and I've got a few to my credit. But I've never had as much satisfaction knowing anyone else was permanently out of commission."

"Yeah, me too." Homes sighed and drained the rest of his beer. It was his fifth. "There's still one little problem, Jack."

"What's that?"

"The chief wants to see me tomorrow. How do I explain all this shit to him?"

"What do you mean?"

"Look at it this way. Here I am, going over to Laura's place with your present in my hands, hoping to catch both of you naked. This nicely dressed guy meets me at the door, and I shoot and kill the son of a bitch. There's no fight or nothing. The guy never even says anything."

"He did have the needle in his hand," Jack said.

"Sure, but I don't know what's in it. For all I know, he's some doctor treating Laura for something. So I walk in and shoot the fucker. How do I explain it all?"

"Well, you saw me lying on the floor."

"Afterward. Afterward, I saw you. Besides, I've seen you plenty of times lying on plenty of floors during your drinking days. All I saw at first was the guy with the needle. I didn't even notice Laura in the chair until after I dropped the bastard."

Jack started laughing hard as he grabbed his friend and hugged him. "Homes, they'll probably throw your ass in the federal pen for this and pipe Bobby Darin records into your cell. Dickens may turn out to be some weird guy who saves orphaned kids or found a cure for cancer."

"Jack, that's not funny, dammit. I'm getting another beer. And then I'm gonna get drunk. And your punishment for being a wiseass is that you have to watch me—and stay sober."

"You're a cruel man, Homes, and a damn good shot."

"You bet your ass."